Vampires
of Ottawa

Books by Eric Wilson

The Tom and Liz Austen Mysteries

1. Murder on *The Canadian*
2. Vancouver Nightmare
3. The Ghost of Lunenburg Manor
4. Disneyland Hostage
5. The Kootenay Kidnapper
6. Vampires of Ottawa
7. Spirit in the Rainforest
8. The Green Gables Detectives
9. Code Red at the Supermall
10. Cold Midnight in Vieux Québec
11. The Ice Diamond Quest
12. The Prairie Dog Conspiracy
13. The St. Andrews Werewolf

Also available by Eric Wilson

Summer of Discovery
The Unmasking of 'Ksan
Terror in Winnipeg
Lost Treasure of Casa Loma

Vampires of Ottawa

Eric Wilson

HarperCollins*PublishersLtd*

First published in hardcover by Collins Publishers: 1984
First paperback edition: 1985

Canadian Cataloguing in Publication Data

Wilson, Eric
    Vampires of Ottawa

(A Liz Austen mystery)
ISBN 0-00-222858-0

I. Title.

PS8595.I4793V36 1985   jC813'.54   C85-099196-X
PZ7.W55Va 1985

---

93 94 95 96 97 98 99 OFF 10 9 8 7 6 5 4 3

Remembering our cat Stripe
He was a good friend

1

They'd put me in a cell on death row.

Thick walls surrounded me. Cold light came through the bars, showing the mattress where I had to sleep. My heart thumped painfully as I thought about the people who had waited in this cell for the sound of approaching feet.

Feet that would lead them to the gallows.

Unable to bear the thought, I sat down on the bare mattress to stare at my suitcase. I felt so homesick. What were Tom and my parents doing right now? Probably drinking hot chocolate and talking about what a great time good old Liz would be having in Ottawa.

They didn't know I'd been condemned to death row.

"Feeling lonely?" a voice said.

Looking up, I saw a teenage girl watching me through the bars of my cell. She had large eyes, a wide mouth and a lot of fuzzy hair that spilled down over her shoulders. With a smile, she opened the cell door. "Feel like a tour of the prison?"

"You bet!"

Anything was better than sitting in that cell alone. Before the girl could change her mind I hurried into the concrete corridor. Blue and green lights shone weakly from the ceiling, and our footsteps echoed as we began walking. This place, called the Nicholas Street Youth Hostel, had once been a prison, but now is a place for travellers to stay. I suppose it may be an adventure for some people to sleep on death row, but I'm not sure I recommend it!

Glancing into the cells gave me the creeps, so I turned to the girl. "My name's Liz Austen. I'm from Winnipeg."

"That's in Alberta?"

"No," I said, annoyed. I'd heard rumours that people in eastern Canada don't know a lot about the west, but this was ridiculous. "Winnipeg is the *capital city* of Manitoba. It's actually quite an advanced place. The roads are paved, and some houses even have electric lights."

The girl looked embarrassed. "Excuse my ignorance, please. I am new to Canada. This country has been my home for only a few months, but I am trying to quickly learn about it."

Now I was the one who felt embarrassed. "Sorry," I mumbled. "I didn't realize ... where are you from?"

"Romania. My name is Orli Yurko."

"I don't believe it! You're actually from Romania?" When she nodded, I smiled happily. "That's where Transylvania is!"

"That's right. It means 'the land beyond the forest.'"

"And it's the home of Dracula. Right?"

"That is true, but ..."

"Wow, Orli, this is so exciting. The reason I'm in Ottawa is to represent Manitoba in the National Public Speaking Contest for schools, and my topic is *Vampires: Do they exist?* You can give me some inside information!"

Orli stared at me suddenly with her large, hazel-coloured eyes. "Not many people my age believe those old superstitions, even in Romania. I'm sorry, Liz, but vampires aren't my sack."

"Aren't your *bag*," I corrected her. "Oh, well, it was a good idea while it lasted."

Orli pushed open a heavy door that led to a stairwell. We started down, our feet clanging against the metal stairs that twisted into the shadows below. "Do you see those heavy metal screens?" Orli asked, pointing at the mesh strung across the stairwell. "Those prevented prisoners from jumping, or from pushing the guards off the stairs."

"Why would anyone jump?"

"They would rather be dead, than led down these stairs to solitary confinement."

"Is that where you're taking me?"

She nodded. "Solitary is the place that scares me the most when I give a tour."

"Do you work in this hostel?"

"Yes. I am an office night-clerk, to earn university money."

"What are you going to study?"

"To be a doctor." Pausing, she pointed at some small windows. "Once a week, families gathered on the other side of those windows. The prisoners were forced to stand here, on the stairs, shouting to their people. That was called a visit."

"That's terrible."

"Solitary was even worse." She led me down a corridor to a row of cells with metal doors. "You see those hatches at the bottom of the doors? Once a day those were opened, to slide inside bread and water. The prisoners lived in darkness that was total. In the winter, no heat. No blankets for them, ever, or even clothes."

"What a *disgusting* way to treat humans. How long were they kept in solitary?"

"Some for one month. And why? Often just because of speaking to another prisoner against rules. But, do you want to know the worst?"

I didn't, but I was too curious to say no.

"Some in solitary were chained to the floor. With molasses poured on their bodies by guards."

"I don't understand."

"The molasses attracted rats. Should I explain more?"

"No! That's just awful, Orli. Thank goodness people are civilized today."

"There's more." Orli took me into a large room filled with tables. "This is now the breakfast room for hostellers. Tomorrow morning you will seat yourself here eating cereal, then go into sunshine and a day of sightseeing. But not long ago, whole families lived in this room and often never left for five years."

"How come?"

"This was called debtors' prison. If a person owed money, and could not pay, then into debtors' prison with him. And his whole family, bringing their furniture along! Mother, father, children, locked in this room because the father owed two dollars and could not pay. This country had savage laws, Liz."

I shook my head, unable to speak.

Orli walked to a door and pointed at a yard surrounded by high walls. "Are cemeteries making you afraid, Liz? Because there is one, where I point." When I looked puzzled, Orli stepped closer. "Mysterious deaths in the prison. Mysterious disappearances. At night, a prisoner asleep in his cell. Perhaps he has caused the guards trouble. In the morning, gone."

"Where to?"

"Since you must know, Liz, I will tell you. Buried in this yard are the bodies of 200 or more. Perhaps some died of natural reasons, but others not. Shall I show you the rope burns?"

For a moment, I hesitated. Why was Orli telling me all this? Why had she suddenly offered to take me on this strange tour of the prison? It was late, and I had to get some sleep. Already I'd heard enough for a week's worth of nightmares, but there was something about Orli that *compelled* me to know more. So, like a fool, I nodded my head. "Sure, let's see the rope burns. I can take it. They grow us tough out west."

With a solemn face, Orli led me through the prison to more stairs. We climbed them in silence, and I confess my heart was thumping pretty hard. Was she leading me into some kind of trap? Orli certainly had a taste for the gruesome. Maybe she was setting me up to become body number 201 in the yard. Of course I knew that was dumb, but I didn't feel any better when I suddenly saw a hangman's rope.

"The gallows!" Orli whispered dramatically. "Now, Liz, listen to me. Your cell is just down that corridor, on death row. Do you know why it is called that?"

"Prisoners sentenced to die are kept in cells on death row."

"Exactly correct. In 1868 a great leader of this nation, Thomas McGee, was shot to death on Sparks Street, Ottawa. Convicted for the crime was a tailor, named Whelan, and for two years he lived on death row. In fact, in the cell that is now *yours*, Liz."

She paused, and I realized my skin was tingling. Orli could sure tell a story. Now she stepped even closer to stare at me with those huge eyes.

"Two years in that cell, Liz. Waiting, waiting, always waiting. At the end, a voice is heard: *James Patrick Whelan, your time has come.* The cell door squeaks open, and Whelan takes the last walk of his life. Down the corridor, to this gallows. Over his head is put a hood. Around his neck, the rope. Liz, it is a terrible moment. A prayer is heard." Orli turned and pointed dramatically at a pedal on the floor. "Slowly, the executioner reaches his foot forward, then pushes down hard on that pedal. With a terrible screech that can be heard by every prisoner on death row, the metal doors beneath Whelan fall open. An agonizing cry as the prisoner drops, and then ... silence."

I stared at her, horrified.

Orli pointed at the stairs we'd just climbed. "Do you see those rope burns in the wooden railing? After the execution, a coffin was lowered on ropes. Inside, the body of James Patrick Whelan, still warm."

"Yuck."

"Reaching the ground floor, the coffin is carried into the yard. And it is buried. Whelan is gone forever."

"What about the other 199 people? Were they all executed, too?"

"Liz, in this prison were only six official executions. Such as Whelan."

"Well, why did the others die?"

Orli stared at me, hard. "Who knows for sure?"

"Well," I said, taking a deep breath. "It's been an interesting evening. I doubt if I'll sleep tonight, but what the heck ..."

"Plenty of time to sleep, once you're in the grave," Orli said solemnly. "Those are the famous words of Benjamin Franklin."

"He must have been a real fun guy."

"Liz, it has been a nice evening for me, but now I say goodbye." Orli looked at me carefully. "Are you a deep sleeper?"

"Normally, but not after this tour."

"Good night, Liz. Don't let the screams bother you."

"*What screams?*" I yelped, but Orli just waved a hand and disappeared down the stairs. Obviously she was just trying to psych me out, to put me into a cold sweat so I'd lie awake all night, staring at the bars of my cell while I waited for the 200 ghosts to rise up from the prison yard and float around my head moaning *Elizabeth Kean Austen, your time has come.* Well, it wasn't going to work!

Whistling cheerfully, I walked down death row. In the darkness of a cell something stirred, then I saw the pale shape of a face. "Will you quit the whistling?" the face mumbled. "I'm trying to sleep."

In another cell, someone was reading in bed. Light from the bare bulb cast long shadows across the corridor as I approached my cell, swung open the bars, and fumbled around arranging my sleeping bag. All the while I kept thinking that James Patrick Whelan had spent two years in this actual cell, waiting and waiting and waiting.

By the time I crawled into the sleeping bag I was feeling pretty grim. I lay with my hands behind my head, my eyes on the ceiling, imagining the sound of the executioner's footsteps approaching along the corridor.

It was a long, long time before I fell asleep. Then, as images of ropes and graves and rats tumbled through my mind, I heard the most horrible sound of my life.

CRASH!!

I knew at once that the metal doors of the gallows had fallen open! I sat up, terrified, as the terrible banging of the doors was followed by a scream that sent fear racing through my body in cold waves. Leaping out of bed, I grabbed my dressing gown and ran into the corridor. Other people were already outside their cells, staring at the door that led to the gallows.

"Don't go down there!" a girl warned as I started walking toward the door. "It sounds as if someone's been executed."

"Don't be dumb," I said, even though my heart was thudding with fear. "Those gallows aren't used anymore."

"Then why do they keep the rope? And, listen, you can still hear those trap doors swinging back and forth. You're crazy! Don't go out there."

Ignoring her, I reached for the handle of the

door and slowly pushed it open. For a moment I was only aware of the powerful lights that had turned the gallows a blood-red colour, and then my heart leapt.

Swinging from the rope was a body.

2

I screamed.

I couldn't stop myself. I screamed and screamed while the body swung back and forth, bathed in the red glow of the lights.

Then I heard hysterical laughter.

Struggling to get my emotions under control, I took a step closer to the gallows and saw Orli hiding near the stairs. Beside her was another teenager. They were both killing themselves laughing. Slowly my brain registered this information. Then I turned my eyes back to the gallows, and realized I had been tricked.

It was only a dummy dangling from the rope. A face had been cleverly painted on it, and a mop had been used for the hair, but the whole "execution" had been a set-up. I had been taken.

Orli and her friend came forward, still laughing.

"No tough feelings, Liz!" Orli said, wiping tears from her eyes. "Sometimes life here is so boring. Do you forgive?"

"That was pretty rough on my nerves."

"I ask for your mercy."

"Okay, Orli. I guess so."

"Liz," she said, looking at me solemnly with those large eyes. "I shall not cause any more trouble in your life."

There was something about the look in her eyes that made me wonder if I could really trust her, and it was a couple of hours before I finally fell asleep. In the morning my eyes had as many red lines as a road map. I had to prop my head in one hand while I sipped orange juice in the breakfast room, but I felt a little more alive when I stepped outside into a brisk wind and cold rain.

With me were the other kids from across Canada who were in Ottawa for the public speaking contest. A couple of them had spent last night on death row, too, so they looked as haggard as me, but everyone else seemed full of energy as our chaperone discussed the plans for our visit.

"Today I'll be showing you some of Ottawa's famous sights. For example," she said, holding up a coin, "how would you like to see one of these actually being made? Or visit a church with a body sealed inside the altar? Tomorrow evening you will give your speeches at Rideau Hall, home of the Governor General. Following that are special tour days before you return home."

A boy held up his hand. "What kind of body is in the altar? A human one?"

The woman nodded. "Follow me and you'll find out."

As our group followed her down Nicholas Street, I leaned close to one of the girls who had also spent the night on death row. "Not another body!" I whispered. "I'll be dead of a heart attack myself before we leave this place."

She smiled. "You sure can scream. My hair actually stood on end last night."

Within a couple of blocks we saw a bronze statue of Terry Fox, leaning into the wind, with rain running down his face like sweat. I got all choked up, especially when I looked at the fresh flowers someone had put in his hand.

"This is a perfect place for Terry Fox," a boy said, looking at the roads that surrounded us. "With all the cars and trucks whizzing past, it's just like when he was running along all those highways."

A few minutes later we saw another statue that got to me. This was the huge war memorial you see on TV every Remembrance Day, showing soldiers abandoning a cannon on the battlefield as they head for home. Maybe I just got a lump in my throat because I was suddenly feeling homesick, but actually I think it was the look on the soldiers' faces. They were such young guys, some of them just boys, but their faces looked old and ruined.

Our guide must have noticed a few gloomy faces, because she made an effort to cheer us up. "It's contest time! Who can spot the world's largest ice rink?"

Before I could even think, some brain had her hand in the air. "The Rideau Canal," she said, pointing at the narrow waterway close by. "In the winter it freezes, and I've heard that people even skate to work carrying their briefcases."

"That's right. It's possible to skate eight kilometres without turning around. In the spring, the banks are lined with tulips given by the people of Holland to thank Canadians for sheltering their Royal Family in Ottawa during the last war."

We saw the Parliament Buildings a few minutes later. I guess I've seen about two million pictures of them, but it's something else to be there in person and see the Peace Tower rising up against the sky. At the top there was a gigantic Canadian flag that our chaperone said is the world's largest. The buildings are stained black, scarred and pitted by age and pollution, but they must have been magnificent when they were first built, with their white walls and copper roofs gleaming in the sun. Bells sounded from the Peace Tower, deep and rolling and peaceful, as we approached.

"Notice the gargoyles," the woman said, pointing at the snarling creatures that leaned out from the walls. "Don't they look like they're guarding the government from attackers?"

Inside, marble ceilings arched high above us, the walls were lined with portraits of Prime Ministers, and there was a feeling of real excitement among the tourists waiting their chance to see the government in action. Nudging the girl beside me, I pointed up at a balcony high above. "Look at that security guard. They're not taking any chances."

"Not after the mad bomber."

"Who?"

"Tell you in a minute," she said, as our line started shuffling forward. We climbed some marble stairs, then went through a metal detector under the eyes of security guards who x-rayed purses and studied everyone carefully.

"See that washroom?" the girl said. "In there a man was putting together a dynamite bomb, to throw at the members of parliament, when something went wrong and the bomb exploded. The washroom door was blown apart, blue smoke poured out, and they found the man dead. He left a note saying he wanted to destroy the government."

"How do you know all this?"

She smiled. "It's part of my speech. I'm also going to talk about the guy who walked into the Québec Legislature with a submachine gun and sprayed bullets around."

"Wow. And I thought vampires was a gruesome topic."

Watched by even more security guards, we went into the gallery and sat down. We were in a huge room, looking down at the MPs who are elected to make the decisions about how Canada is run. They sat at desks with green tops, listening to a blond man giving a speech. He was very good looking in his cream-coloured suit. After a while, I let my eyes roam around, looking for famous faces.

"There's one," I said, pointing at a young woman with long hair. "I saw her on TV talking about oil wells."

"Here comes the Prime Minister!" the girl beside me said. "Look at that tan."

Everyone in the gallery leaned forward, whispering, as the Prime Minister walked to his desk. He wore a dark suit with a red tie, had a slim body and greying hair swept back from his face.

I was pretty impressed, especially after he delivered a speech, switching effortlessly between English and French. After he finished, some MPs at other desks wrote him notes, which were delivered by messengers no older than me.

"What a great job," I whispered, watching the young pages with envy. "Wouldn't it be neat to be so close to all those powerful people?"

Shortly after, we left the Parliament Buildings and discovered glorious sunshine pouring down through holes torn in the clouds by a strong wind. Warm light glowed from the copper roofs of the many towers and turrets that made the nearby Chateau Laurier Hotel look just like a European castle as we headed for Lower Town to eat beaver tails, which are crispy pastries covered with sugar and cinnamon. I was still licking my lips when we got to the Basilica Notre-Dame, where the body of Saint Felicity is sealed inside the high altar, and then we continued on to the Mint to see money being made.

What a place it was. The racket was tremendous as huge presses punched out blank coins before sending them to other machines for stamping on the designs. I was impressed by a device that counts twenty-five thousand coins in one minute, but what I liked best were the bins full of coins that looked so strange because they were totally blank. I was kind of hoping for free samples of a few dollars when we left the Mint, but no such luck!

The best part of the day was the RCMP musical ride, which I'd only seen in pictures. We only saw a practice session, but even that was a real thrill for a horse freak like me. I could have spent hours watching the black horses and their riders in the ring. They formed circles and figure eights, at the trot and canter, while their hooves kicked up dirt and little birds flew around in the steel girders high above. Sunshine slanted in, lighting up the flags of all the countries where the musical ride has appeared, and I practically drooled with envy as I thought about travelling the world as one of those riders.

By the time I got home to death row, I was feeling really good. Of course, I didn't have any idea then what would happen the next day on the river. If I'd known, I guess I wouldn't have been in such a good mood. In fact, I'd have been shivering in my shoes.

3

Everything started with the river tour.

Actually, it was really pleasant at first. It was a hot day for September, so I was wearing shorts and a t-shirt. The sun warmed my back as I leaned over the railing of the cruise boat, watching waves splash away from the bow and talking to Orli. She had invited me to take this river tour as her guest. Maybe it was her way of apologizing for the trick with the dummy.

As the boat headed out on the river I recognized a famous scene that's on lots of Ottawa travel posters.

"Orli, do you see that building that looks like a wedding cake? It's the government library, and our guide told us yesterday that it's the only survivor of the big fire of 1916 that wiped out the original Parliament Buildings. Boy, people are strange. Did you know that two women were killed when they ran back inside to get their fur coats? Imagine running into a burning building for a coat!"

Orli gazed out over the water. "For some people, money and possessions are everything, Liz. Especially if they have been poor all their lives ..."

For a while we didn't say anything else, just relaxed and enjoyed the scenery. The Gatineau hills were lovely with all the leaves turning to reds and oranges and yellows, and I liked the sight of the church spires rising above the little houses on the far shore of the river. Lots of boats were out, taking advantage of the sunshine, while tugs passed with their log booms. Meanwhile, a voice over the cruise boat's loudspeaker described the enormous houses we saw on shore, like 24 Sussex Drive where the Prime Minister lives.

"Do you miss Romania, Orli?"

She sighed. "Many times, Liz, especially my friends. But the life of Canada is good, and now I would miss Ottawa if I left."

"What did you do for fun there? Watch TV?"

"Not many people have television, and that included us. Instead we hiked in the mountains, or danced to gypsy music."

"No rock?"

"Sure!" she said, laughing. "But not the fancy stereo systems. People have not much money for stereos or cars. It would take three years of saving all money from work to buy a car."

"Is that why you moved to Canada?"

She nodded. "There are only three in my family. Me, mother and my uncle. He has a bad sickness, but no money for treating him. So mother and I came to Canada, and she saves money that will help him."

"What does she do?"

"It's very exciting! In Romania, she had a famous name for cooking. One day, she was invited to move to Ottawa and become chef for a very wealthy man. His name is Baron Nicolai Zaba. As a young man, he moved here from Romania. Those were good times, and he prospered. Much money came to him."

"Wait a minute. Is he the one who owns the big pulp and paper mills?"

"The same."

"But that company is all over North America! He must be a zillionaire."

"Perhaps," she smiled. "Or maybe only a trillionaire."

"I'd like to meet that man. Maybe he's in the market for a bride."

"Funny you should mention that, Liz. The Baron announced his engagement recently. The marriage is soon."

"Wow. Who's the lucky girl?"

"Her name is Dionne. She met him only a few months ago. She is younger than the Baron by several years, but they seem to be very much in love."

I sighed. "How romantic. Are you invited to the wedding?"

"Yes, and I will sprinkle salt on the bride's head."

"I'll bet that's for good luck. Listen, maybe you

could send me a slice of the wedding cake to put under my pillow."

"For what reason?"

"Then I'll dream of the man I'm going to marry." For a few minutes I watched the shimmering of the sunshine on the waves, and listened to the pleasant rumble of the diesel engine from below decks. Then my thoughts were interrupted by Orli pointing to shore.

"We are approaching Blackwater Estate, the home of Baron Zaba. Do you see that boathouse? It belongs to the Baron, as do all the lands along the river. Just above the trees you see the tower, which is a part of the mansion where I live."

"Hey, you actually *live* there?"

"Certainly, Liz. Mama and I have rooms. It is very pleasant."

"I'd love to visit."

She smiled. "Perhaps it would be possible. I will ask."

At that moment, a deckhand shouted. The sound was so unexpected and so loud that everyone along the railing almost jumped out of their skins. Then we turned and saw the deckhand pointing at a woman in the water.

She was between us and the shore, and swimming our way. When she stopped to wave for help, there was panic all over her face. "She's drowning!" someone shouted.

Loud clangs sounded from the bridge as the captain signalled for the boat to be stopped. Deckhands scrambled toward one of the lifeboats and began the process of lowering it, but they seemed to take forever and I started getting really frightened. The woman wasn't a very good swimmer, and she seemed to be swallowing a lot of water.

Then I saw the man.

He appeared suddenly on a small dock connected to the boathouse on shore. He was too far away for me to see his face, but I saw him dive into the water. I felt relieved to see someone going to the rescue. But when the woman saw him coming her way, she did a strange thing.

She started swimming away from the man.

At the same moment, one of the deckhands swore loudly. "The lifeboat's jammed!" he yelled to the captain. "We can't move it."

"Lower another one! But hurry. She's getting weak."

Again the woman had stopped swimming, and was waving to us for help. The man was still coming her way, but I didn't think he'd reach her before she went under for good.

"Hold these," I said to Orli, handing her my camera and purse. Quickly I kicked off my sandals. Climbing onto the railing, I took a deep breath and then arced out over the river in a low dive. The cold water gave me a shock as I sliced beneath the surface. Within seconds my skin was numb, and I was swimming toward the woman as quickly as possible.

She saw me coming. For a moment I thought she'd panic and try to get away from me, too, but then I saw how exhausted she was. I wanted to yell at her to hang on but I knew that wouldn't help, so I concentrated all my energy on reaching her before she went under.

I got to her just in time. She had no strength left. I got one arm around her body, and kept her head above the surface while I waited for the lifeboat. She kept moaning and mumbling, but I couldn't make out the words. I just kept telling her she was safe.

"We're coming," a voice called. Then I heard the putter of the lifeboat's engine.

Within a minute the woman had been lifted to safety and I was being helped aboard the lifeboat. Once aboard, I looked around for the strange man, but he was nowhere to be seen. Who was he? There was something weird about the way the woman had swum from him in panic, when she should have waited for his help.

The lifeboat turned around and started heading back to the cruise boat, and I squinted back to the dock. As I looked up at the boathouse window, I thought I could see the pale shape of a face watching from the shadows.

When we were back on the cruise ship, the ship's crew took care of the woman and Orli wrapped a blanket around my shoulders.

"Thanks, Orli. I'm freezing." My teeth were chattering, and I was thankful when the ship got under way, heading for home. "Listen, did you know that man in the water? Have you seen him before at the Baron's estate?"

"My eyes are not good, Liz. From here, he was just looking like a blur."

"What about the woman?"

Orli bit her lip. "Her I do know, Liz."

"Well? Who is she?"

"She is the fiancée of the Baron! The woman he will marry."

I could hardly believe it.

"Where is she?" I asked, suddenly forgetting how cold I was. Orli pointed toward the cabin on the boat's upper deck.

Sunshine streamed into the cabin, lighting the anxious faces of the people huddled around the Baron's fiancée. Several cushions had been removed from chairs to make a bed, and she lay under a heap of blankets. Her skin was terribly pale and her eyes were closed, but they opened when I knelt down beside her.

"The vampire!" she cried, her whole body trembling. "Please, save me!"

4

Those words completely freaked me.

Most people never think twice about vampires. They think they're just made-up movie characters like Dracula — guys with fangs and black capes who go around cackling their heads off and drinking people's blood. I knew that Dracula had been a real person — Vlad the Impaler — and once I started researching material for my speech, I was even more convinced that people could rise up from the grave.

I stared unbelievingly at the Baron's fiancée as she moaned about vampires. Some of the other people said she was just having nightmares, but her eyes were wide open. She kept staring at *me*, almost as if she knew how I felt about the undead, until finally the boat reached its dock and ambulance attendants came on board to take her to hospital.

Orli looked worried as she watched the stretcher being carried to the ambulance. "She has suffered a terrible shock, Liz. I hope she will live! The Baron would be in anguish to lose her."

"I wonder why she was in the river? I'm sure she was trying to escape from that man."

"No, Liz. I am certain he just wanted to help."

I wasn't at all sure of this, and secretly I wished I could do some investigating around the boathouse, where I'd seen that strange man. All afternoon I tried to figure out why the Baron's fiancée would be so scared of vampires, but then I gave up. I was getting nervous about vampires, too. Soon, I'd be giving a speech about them!

In the evening a special bus arrived at the youth hostel to take all the contestants to Rideau Hall, where we would give our speeches. On the way, the woman who was hosting the event stood at the front of the bus, telling us about our destination.

"Rideau Hall is the home of the Governor General. She is Commander in Chief of the armed forces, she can call an election for a new government, and she must sign all new laws. That makes her the most powerful person in Canada, but I think you will like her very much."

The girl beside me, whose name was Carolyn, held up her hand. "Are we actually going to meet the Governor General?"

"That's right. After the speeches, she's giving

a reception for you in the Tent Room of Rideau Hall. It's quite a house, you know. There are more than 100 rooms, lots of chandeliers, Chinese furniture, and a private garden with its own totem pole." She looked out the window. "We're almost there. That big house across the street is 24 Sussex Drive. Imagine having the Prime Minister as your neighbour!"

As our bus entered the gates of Rideau Hall, a Mountie on guard duty saluted us. I looked out at the huge grounds. "Is it true that the Governor General has her own private hockey rink?"

"That's right, plus a toboggan slide and a cricket pitch for the summer. The Governor General has practically an entire village here, in fact, because there's a fire hall and a church and an RCMP office. Those trees you see were planted by queens and kings and presidents, while they were here, sleeping over as guests. On the grounds are lots of sugar maples, which are tapped to make the maple syrup eaten in Rideau Hall."

"Fantastic!" a boy said. "Can we stay for breakfast?"

Everyone laughed, which helped us relax, but I was feeling *very* solemn as we got off the bus. "My mouth's gone dry," I whispered to Carolyn. "I'll probably faint in the middle of my speech."

A man in elegant clothes opened the front door of Rideau Hall. The entrance hall was huge, with a wide staircase covered in a carpet so red it practically blinded my eyes. There was carved marble everywhere, and on the cream-coloured walls were portraits of royalty.

We smoothed our skirts, and the boys adjusted their ties, and then we climbed those wide steps to be shown into the ballroom. At first I was stunned by its size, then by the chandelier that glittered and glistened above us, then by the carpet which seemed as big as a football field. But mostly, I confess, I was surprised at how many people were sitting in the fancy chairs.

"Is all this for us?" I said to Carolyn, as the people smiled and applauded. "Or do you think the Edmonton Oilers are coming, too?"

"I think it's just for us," she said, gulping. "And I think I'm going to throw up."

The applause continued as we were led to the front of the ballroom, where velvet chairs had been reserved for us. Some special guests were introduced, but I didn't catch their names because I was trembling like a leaf caught between two hurricanes. *What am I doing here?* I moaned to myself as powerful lights were switched on for the television cameras, and the first contestant went to the microphone.

I don't think I heard a single word of his speech. I remember that his lips moved, and I'm sure I heard laughter from the audience, but I spent the whole time hating my parents for landing me with Austen for a name. Why? Because we were speaking in alphabetical order, and that meant I was next.

"And now," the master of ceremonies said cheerfully, "a speech with a difference. Representing the province of Manitoba, may I present Elizabeth Austen."

Somehow I managed to stand up. Somehow I managed to get to the microphone. Somehow I kept from flinching as a flash camera exploded in my face. But my voice sounded like Minnie Mouse when I started talking.

"My topic," I squeaked, then stopped to clear my throat. "My topic is vampires." This produced some laughter, but then people seemed to realize I was serious, and they settled back to listen politely as I talked about how people all over the world believed in vampires. For example, in Africa there is the *asanbosam*, a vampire who sucks blood from the thumbs of sleeping people, and the Chinese never allowed a cat into the same room as the body of a dead person, because if the cat jumped over the coffin, they believed that person would become a vampire.

Some people have tried to explain the vampire legends by saying that during the Black Death, victims were often buried alive in the haste to get them below ground. If these coffins were later opened, they often showed signs of vampirism such as blood on their bodies, caused by the victims tearing their own flesh in attempts to free themselves.

By now I could see that my audience was getting hooked. I talked about international vampire superstitions, and soon they were leaning forward in their chairs. "The Ruthenians gather thorn branches and place them on the threshold of their houses as protection, but most people prefer to use garlic. In Romania windows are rubbed with garlic, and bundles of it are hung around windows and doors."

Finally I paused, and looked around the sumptuous ballroom with its high windows and gold-trimmed ceiling. "Ladies and gentlemen," I said. "Do vampires exist today? Until someone proves otherwise, I believe they might. Please let me suggest, therefore, that you sleep with garlic close by your bed!"

As the audience applauded, I returned to my seat. It was over! Carolyn leaned close to whisper her congratulations, then her name was announced. Looking relaxed and confident, she launched into a speech about the Olympic movement that I thought could easily take first prize.

Sure enough, when the judges announced their decision later that night it was Carolyn who stood up to receive the cheers of the audience. I guess I was a bit disappointed, because I'd had fantasies about arriving home at Winnipeg airport carrying a gold trophy, but Carolyn really deserved to win.

Then we went to the reception. What an experience that was! We stood in a long line, waiting our turn to meet the Governor General and her husband. Each of us had been given a card with our name printed on it, and we handed this to an *aide de camp*, who read our name to a second *aide* who then introduced us to the Governor General. She was a handsome white-haired woman with a fantastic smile, but all I can remember about our meeting was that when we shook hands, mine was dripping sweat, I was so nervous.

The rest of the evening was fun. The reception was held in the Tent Room, which has been lined with candy-striped canvas ever since the last century, when a Governor General built the room as an indoor tennis court.

I was gorging myself on spicy apple juice and a plate piled high with food, when one of the other contestants came up to congratulate me on my speech.

"Boy, you sure have a taste for the gruesome," she laughed. Then she squinted at me curiously. "But nobody really *believes* in vampires anymore, do they?"

I thought about Baron Zaba's fiancée, and suddenly a chill of fear passed through me. Maybe most people didn't believe in vampires, but the Baron's fiancee sure did.

And I did, too.

5

Simon Sharples entered my life the next day.

I first saw him behind the wheel of a limousine that must have been a block long. Chrome and black paint gleamed in the evening sun, the whitewalls were dazzling, and the smoked-glass windows looked mysterious and glamorous, but my eyes saw only the driver.

He was gorgeous. Tall, with black hair in soft waves, dark eyes and a rugged face. I was practically drooling as I watched him go to the limo's rear door and open it. He didn't just walk, but moved like a tiger slinking through the jungle.

"Who *is* he?" I whispered to Orli. We stood together outside the youth hostel, dressed in our best clothes, wearing corsages that threw off a sweet fragrance. The corsages were a gift of the Baron, and so were the tickets we held to see "Swan Lake" that evening. It was his way of thanking us for helping to save the life of his fiancée.

"Simon Sharples is the chauffeur of the Baron," Orli said curtly. "And believe me, Liz, he knows how handsome he is. He has been told he could make a great deal of money as a model or actor, but for some reason he will not leave the Baron."

Hoping I wasn't acting like a simp, I walked to the limo and got inside. As I did, I gave Simon Sharples my very best, my very sweetest, smile. He didn't seem to notice, but so what! At least I'd been close enough to gaze into those perfect eyes.

The limo smelled of leather and plush velvet. Under my feet was a thick carpet. There was almost enough room for a swimming pool, and I stared in amazement at the wood panelling and the TV set before turning to the woman who was already in the limo.

"Hi, I'm Liz Austen."

"Please call me Jayne." She was about 40, showing the first grey in her short black hair, and wearing earrings that I first thought were diamonds before deciding they must be cut-glass. Her long blue dress was pretty but kind of frilly and out of date, and a bit shiny at the elbows. I know it sounds like I was examining her with a fine-toothed comb, but I also couldn't help noticing a run in her stockings. She looked a little tense. Jayne turned to me with a smile, which briefly removed the frown from between her eyes. Then once again her face looked strained. "I am Personal Assistant to the Baron, so he asked me to escort you to the ballet. Are you enjoying Ottawa?"

"Yes, and Orli has been wonderful to me. How is the Baron's fiancée today?"

"Still in hospital, and still in serious condition." Jayne looked out the smoked glass at the people and buildings slipping past as we sped along city streets. Not a single sound entered from outside to disturb us. "She seems to have had a terrible shock. Her experience in the river seems to have weakened Dionne more than we had thought, and the doctors say she keeps raving about vampires, which seems strange as she is such a level-headed woman."

"Maybe vampires do exist."

"Rubbish." She looked at me sharply.

The word stung. I felt my face going red, and turned to look out the window. Maybe Jayne was feeling uptight about something, but I wasn't going to let that spoil my big evening at the ballet. As the limo pulled into the driveway of the National Arts Centre I leaned forward in excitement.

"Wow! Look at all the tuxedos and long dresses!"

Jayne smiled at me. "You and Orli also look lovely. You'll be a great success."

"Thank you," I said, softening toward her. "But I wish I'd had time to wash my hair. I look like a bride of Dracula!"

It was supposed to be a joke, but it bombed. The creases deepened on Jayne's face, and she gave me a strange look before reaching for a phone. "After you park the limousine, Simon, please join us inside. We'll wait in the foyer." As she hung up, I goggled in amazement.

"Can you phone anywhere on that thing? Even to Winnipeg?"

"Certainly. Would you care to try?"

"No, thanks," I said, shaking my head. "Next you're going to tell me this limo has concealed submachine guns."

"No, but it would be impossible for anyone to fire bullets *into* here." She rapped the window with her knuckles. "This glass is six centimetres thick. Even a bazooka shell would bounce off."

"Wow! Has the Baron ever been attacked?"

Jayne shook her head. "But, like all wealthy people, he has certain fears."

"Such as ..?"

"I don't think that's any of your business."

"Sorry," I mumbled, feeling my face turn red again. "I guess I'm too nosy."

"Remember, Liz, curiosity killed the cat."

Simon Sharples held the door open for us. As I stepped out of the car I tried to flutter my eyelashes his way, but then I was blinded by the flashing of cameras. For a moment I wondered if I was the star of the show, but Orli brought me back to earth in a hurry.

"The news reporters are just warming up their cameras. In a few minutes is the arrival of the Prime Minister."

"Hey, I'd like to see that!"

Jayne looked at her watch. "There should be time. Besides, we have to wait for Simon to park the car."

Our limo powered silently away, and then another black monster rolled into the driveway. This one was so long I didn't know how the driver could get it around corners.

The Prime Minister's wife stepped out first, all her jewellery winking and blinking in the glare of TV lights. She was tall and dark, really beautiful, but the Prime Minister was just as good looking in his black tuxedo with a red flower on the lapel. They didn't seem to mind the constant flashing of cameras. They just stood smiling and waving to the crowds behind rope barricades, then went inside holding hands. Surrounding them were some tough-looking men and women, who stared suspiciously at everyone.

"Top security!" I whispered to Orli.

Inside the theatre people were stretching their necks, trying to get a look at the PM and his wife. I could see, in one part of the lobby, a lot of white tablecloths holding silver candlesticks and crystal goblets, so I asked Jayne if they were going to eat dinner.

She shook her head. "After tonight's performance, there will be a gala reception for the ballet troupe. People will be served pâté and shrimp sandwiches, and all the ladies will receive a tiny bottle of Chanel No. 5, but of course the big treat will be a chance to chat with the Prime Minister and his wife."

"Are we going?" I asked hopefully.

"No such luck."

"But the Baron is a big cheese in this country. Why didn't he get an invitation?"

"He did, actually, but had to say no. His poor health means he cannot leave Blackwater Estate, even to visit his fiancée in hospital. The Baron has had several severe heart attacks, and the doctors have warned him to avoid any strain whatsoever. They are very worried. Another heart attack may kill the man."

I know it sounds tacky, but I couldn't help wondering who would inherit the Baron's money if he died. Obviously his fiancée would get it, but what if something happened before they were able to marry? I was dying to ask Jayne, but I already knew what her response would be. Forget it!

I looked around the lobby. The walls were kind of dark, but just above us was a bright tapestry showing native hunters in pursuit of wolves, who were baring their teeth and looking savage. Dracula would envy those teeth, I thought, but again I didn't say anything to Jayne. For some reason, the subject of vampires seemed to make her particularly tense.

Several diplomat-looking types stood close by. I couldn't understand a single word they were saying, so I turned my ears to a nearby couple who were speaking English. Then, like so many people I'd overheard in Ottawa, they switched easily to French ... just as I switched my eyes to the front door.

Simon Sharples had walked in. Heads turned as people watched him cross the lobby, looking glorious in his tuxedo. Why *didn't* he try his luck in Hollywood?

Jayne looked at her watch. "Trouble parking, Simon?"

For the first time I heard his voice, which made me think of rich chocolate milk, don't ask me why. "Really, Jayne, you're terribly moody lately."

"I'm sorry," she answered, although she didn't look sorry. Instead she seemed nervous, biting a fingernail as she watched the Prime Minister and his wife talking to an African wearing a robe of swirling oranges and yellows.

"Biting yourself is an unattractive habit, Jayne. Remember, you represent the Baron, so conduct yourself accordingly."

"Simon, I've been with the Baron for many years. I've no need for advice from you." Taking a step closer, she put all four fingers into her mouth at once, staring defiantly at him while she slowly chewed. Then she turned to me and smiled. "Simon and I have our differences, but at heart we love each other."

Simon snorted. "I'm going to my seat," he said, and walked away.

"He's *so* good-looking," I whispered to Jayne. "Are you two married or something?"

Instead of answering, she laughed so loudly that nearby people turned to stare. Then she put an arm around my shoulders. "Liz, thank you for the best laugh I've had in weeks. Believe me, I needed that."

"What's so funny?"

"Nothing," she said, chuckling. "Come on, let's go sit down."

Jayne certainly had a knack for making me feel dumb. I rolled my eyes at Orli, then we went into the theatre. It was dominated by spectacular curtains of red velvet, which I stared at as we walked down a crimson carpet to our seats. On the wall were lights in star-burst patterns, and high above was a brilliant sun. Everything was so luxurious that I almost felt like a fairy princess at a ball, so you can imagine how pleased I was when I realized I'd be sitting beside Prince Charming himself, the one and only Simon Sharples.

Not that it turned out to be one of my finer moments. He didn't even glance my way as I sat down, just went on reading his program. I listened for a minute to the weird sounds rising from the orchestra pit, where all the instruments clashed with each other as the players warmed up. Then I turned to Simon. "Do you like ballet?"

"That's why I'm here," he said, keeping right on reading.

"Do you have a favourite company?"

"Ballet isn't the same as football, young lady. I don't cheer for Sadler's Wells, or hiss at the Bolshoi. Each company has its strengths, and should be appreciated for that reason, and that reason alone."

Wow! This guy sure was touchy, but I don't give up easily. "The Royal Winnipeg Ballet is special to me, Simon, because I'm from Winnipeg."

"We all have our problems."

It was about the rudest remark I'd ever heard, and I stared angrily at Simon, expecting him to apologize, or even make a joke out of it. Instead, he just went on staring at his program. I simmered for a few minutes, then got distracted when the Prime Minister and his wife appeared on a white balcony above us. As they smiled and waved before sitting down, I leaned close to Jayne. "They seem to really like each other."

She nodded, and I noticed how she touched her shiny gold wedding ring. "There is nothing stronger than a marriage built on true love."

"Your ring's so shiny, I guess you haven't been married long."

"Absolutely correct!"

"What's your husband like?"

"He makes me laugh! He has a wonderful sense of humour, and we spend hours giggling together over the silliest things." For a moment she smiled to herself, then I saw the happiness slide off her face. "Of course, it was nice to finally receive a marriage proposal, at age 40, but I married for love."

"I'm sure he did, too."

"I hope so," she said, sounding a bit sad, "although I wasn't always certain. Before we married he did ask me about the inheritance I was to receive, but as it turns out I won't be getting the money. I'm happy to say that my husband still seems to love me dearly." She smiled. "I've already noticed how observant you are, Liz, so I'm sure you've figured out that this is not exactly a high-paying job."

"But the Baron is loaded! Why can't he pay you a decent salary?"

Jayne frowned, and said sharply, "I have no complaints. It's interesting work, and the Baron is very kind. I certainly couldn't have afforded to go to the ballet, and Swan Lake is one of my favourites. Have you heard about this production of Sadler's Wells? I understand it's very unusual."

Before I could answer, the lights began to dim. There was a burst of applause as the orchestra conductor appeared, followed by a few seconds of program-rattling and coughing from the audience before the theatre was filled by the clear, sweet note of a wind instrument. It was thrilling to hear the strings join in, then see the velvet curtains sweep up to reveal the stage.

But what a shock I received. I'd been expecting the ballet's usual opening scene of happy young men hunting in the woods, but instead there was a funeral procession crossing the stage, with mourners dressed entirely in black escorting the coffin of the king. A jewelled crown was on top of the coffin. A chill went through me, because any superstitious person will tell you it's bad luck to attend a funeral unless you've been invited. Maybe being in a theatre audience doesn't really count, but I still felt scared.

Things didn't get any more cheerful. The ballet tells the story of an enchanted princess who has been transformed into a swan by an evil magician, and can only return to human form at night. She falls in love with a prince, who vows his love, but then blows it when the magician tricks him into falling for another girl. Instead of the princess being freed from the spell to marry the prince, they are trapped, and can only unite their love for eternity by drowning together in the lake.

It's a really tragic story, and it made me cry. The entire production was as gloomy as the opening funeral scene, with people in black cloaks lurking around bleak castles and in dark woods, so I got more and more depressed until the final scene, which just about pushed me over the edge. The prince, before jumping into the lake, managed to get his revenge by ripping off the magician's helmet, the source of his evil power. Suddenly the stage went black, then we saw only the magician's white face.

It looked like a death's head, with a black mouth and staring black eyes, and I watched in horror as the magician staggered around the stage, then died.

I was totally freaked. The curtains dropped, the dancers came forward for their bows while the audience shouted bravos, but I hardly noticed because my mind was filled with the image of that death's head.

Finally I realized Jayne was shaking my arm. "What's wrong, Liz?"

I could barely speak. "That last scene ... with the head ..."

"Did the magician's face make you think of Dracula?"

I turned to her, surprised. "How did you know?"

"Perhaps ..." she hesitated, "perhaps it was a lucky guess." Again she hesitated. "Would you tell me about your interest in vampires?"

I launched into a summary of my speech, but I got the impression she was only waiting for a chance to ask a particular question. Sure enough, as soon as I paused she jumped right in. "But, Liz, do you actually *believe* in vampires?"

"Let's just say I keep a supply of garlic and wooden stakes handy. Not that I've needed them, but why take chances?" I shrugged. "Of course, my brother Tom thinks I'm totally out to lunch. So do a lot of people, but I can't help that."

Jayne studied me intently, then nodded. "You're strange for a modern girl. But I'd advise you not to let your imagination run away with you."

Again I felt my face turn red. For a few minutes I'd actually started to like Jayne, but now once more I was left feeling like a dumb kid. I was also left with a big question mark hanging over my head.

Why was everyone suddenly so interested in vampires?

6

Blackwater Estate.

For days I'd wondered what it was like, but I had no idea I would actually visit the home of Baron Nicolai Zaba. Then, the day after seeing Swan Lake, I received a phone call from Orli.

"You are invited to be a guest at Blackwater, Liz! Pack your suitcase, for the limousine collects you in 30 minutes."

"Orli, that's fantastic, but why me?"

"For thanking you, I suppose, in helping with the rescue in the river."

I said I was pleased, but secretly I sensed there was something weird about this invitation, and wondered if I should decline. But I'm the courageous type, and I was curious to see Blackwater and maybe meet the Baron. I also knew this would be my chance to investigate the boathouse, and maybe find out more about the mysterious man who had chased the Baron's fiancée. So I got permission from our group's chaperone, and soon was whistling cheerfully as I packed up my things. I was feeling so good I even thought I might miss my cell on death row. As I waited outside for the limo my curiosity about Blackwater grew stronger, until I remembered what Jayne had said to me yesterday:

Remember, Liz, curiosity killed the cat.

I shivered suddenly. Why did that woman make me feel so on edge? When the limousine pulled up I was glad to see that she wasn't inside, and then I was really pleased when I realized I'd be all alone with Simon Sharples. As soon as I'd sunk down into the luxurious seat, and we'd pulled away from the youth hostel, I picked up the telephone.

"Thanks for coming to get me, Simon."

He reached for his phone, and those gorgeous eyes looked at me in the rear-view mirror. "That's what I was ordered to do."

"Wasn't the ballet sumptuous? I thought they danced with such *éclat*." I figured Simon would be impressed by that million-dollar word, which I'd rehearsed carefully to get the pronounciation right, but he didn't even seem to hear.

Instead, he hung up the phone.

I don't give up easily, so I reached for the power-window control switch. Silently the glass partition between me and Simon rolled down, and I was free to speak without using the phone.

"Have you worked for the Baron for long, Simon?" When there was no reply, I pressed bravely on. "It's so nice of him to invite me to Blackwater."

"It wasn't the Baron's idea. Since those heart attacks, he's been under the thumb of his valet. That odious little snob thinks he runs Blackwater."

"What's a valet?"

"He's the personal servant to Baron Zaba. They spend all their time together, so it's no wonder that Lobos can control the Baron."

"Lobos? What a weird name."

"He's a weird man." Simon sank into a moody silence, and said nothing more as we left the downtown streets behind and raced north along a wide boulevard. Occasionally I glimpsed the river, looking dark and angry under the black skies that threatened rain, and I shivered when I remembered the Baron's fiancée swimming for her life.

"Do you like swimming, Simon?"

For a second his perfect face was changed by the appearance of a smile, but it was the coldest smile I've ever seen. "Sure I like swimming, but I don't see that it's any of your business. You people from the boonies seem pretty nosy."

"*The boonies*?" I said angrily. "Are you referring to Winnipeg?"

He laughed, "That's right, little lady."

That did it. I reached for the control switch, and watched the glass partition slide up to cut off Simon Sharples. As it did, I vowed never to speak to the man again, so I ignored him when he picked up his phone shortly after and buzzed me.

I got great satisfaction in pretending I didn't hear, but I was surprised and disappointed when the partition rolled smoothly down. Obviously Simon could control it, too. "Fooled you, eh?" he said with a cool smile. I didn't say a word, but he kept talking anyway. "We're now approaching Blackwater Estate. It's so old that nobody knows the history, but there's talk it was once a lunatic asylum. I think the Baron has been acting so strangely lately because there are still bad vibrations in the air from the days of the asylum."

My ears perked up. "What do you mean?"

"Gotcha!" Simon exclaimed, laughing gleefully. "I knew you were giving me the silent treatment, but nobody gets the best of Simon Sharples. Understand?"

It took all my strength to stare without flinching at those dark eyes reflected in the rear-view mirror. How could a man look so good and act so mean?

Turning off the boulevard, we followed a road through thick woods. Trees pressed so close around that they blocked out the weak light from the dark sky. The interior of the limousine became very gloomy and I hugged my body, feeling strangely cold. When an iron gate appeared ahead I expected Simon to stop, but he kept right on moving at full speed. I cringed back in my seat, waiting for the crash, then saw the gate swing open at the last second.

With that hair-raising introduction, I arrived at Blackwater Estate.

Thick woods continued to surround us for several minutes. Then we drove into an area that resembled a giant park. Formal gardens with magnificent displays of flowers were everywhere. There were wide lawns with grass so green I didn't think it could be real, and water shot from the mouth of a sea serpent at the top of a tall fountain. In the distance I could see the house itself, and again I shivered.

Unlike the gardens and lawns, which were cheerful, the house looked like something out of a horror movie. The walls were black with age and covered with ivy that seemed to be choking them, while the small windows squinted like suspicious eyes hiding secrets. Above the house rose the circular tower which I remembered seeing from the river. At that moment lightning flicked across the black sky, followed by the rumble of thunder. Next came rain, lashing suddenly down as if a giant hand had torn open the clouds.

The limousine stopped under a wide roof in front of the house. Jayne was waiting by the massive oak door, looking very business-like in a suit and white blouse. She came down the stone steps as I stepped from the limousine. "Welcome to Blackwater, Liz. I was surprised, and glad, to hear you'd been invited to stay as our guest." She was smiling, but when she got closer I could see an unusual look in her eyes.

"Let's go inside." Jayne took me firmly by the elbow. "Simon will put your suitcase in the burgundy room. I selected that room especially for you."

"Where's Orli?"

"You'll see her shortly, but first the Baron wants to meet you, and so does my husband."

"I'm looking forward to meeting your husband. He sounds like a great guy."

"How long can you stay, Liz? He wants to know."

"Only a couple of days. The rest of the kids in our group are going to Montreal before we all fly

home, but I got permission to visit here instead."
There was a crack of thunder, and even more
rain smashed down on Blackwater. Bad weather
or not, I couldn't wait to investigate the boathouse and the man in the river. But I didn't tell
Jayne this. Instead I asked about the Baron's
fiancée.

Jayne shook her head. "She's still not well
enough to leave the hospital." She sighed. "The
poor woman. She only met Baron Zaba recently,
and for some reason her life seems to have been
rough ever since."

"Has the Baron been to see her?"

"No. His heart is so weak that the doctors
won't let him leave his suite of rooms in this
house."

I smiled. "You may call it a house, but I'd say
it's a mansion. I bet there's at least 50 rooms."

"I've never counted."

As we approached the oak door, I noticed a
brass knocker shaped like a little man, all curled
up with a pipe in his hands and an evil grin on
his face. His beady eyes actually seemed to be
watching me. It gave me the creeps as I entered
the house.

I'd been half expecting it to be something out
of *The Curse of Frankenstein*, with cold winds
howling down stone passages and rats scuttling
away into darkened corners, so I was surprised
to find myself in a hallway with beautiful white
carpeting, pretty blue-and-gold wallpaper and
antique furniture that glowed under the soft
light of a chandelier. Nearby, a silver bowl containing white roses stood on a polished mahogany table.

Jayne led me into a room about the size of a
hockey rink, and also beautifully furnished.
"Isn't that Ormolu clock exquisite?" she asked,

indicating a delicate timepiece ticking on the mantel above a fireplace faced with Dutch tiles. "The Baron has an outstanding collection of antiques. Many of the chairs in this room are cushioned in Utrecht velvet, and just look at that ottoman. Craftsmanship at its finest." She stroked the carved wooden back of an antique chair almost lovingly. Her eyes glowed.

As she showed me a cabinet containing a collection of Waterford glass I realized I was beginning to relax about being at Blackwater. Then I happened to walk over to some tall French doors that opened onto an area behind the house.

"Good grief! There's a whole cemetery out there."

"Don't worry," Jayne said, coming to stand beside me. "It hasn't been used for years."

"That doesn't make me feel any better."

"We believe this estate may have been a lunatic asylum long ago. I've studied those old tombstones, and I think the people buried in the cemetery were patients of the asylum. They probably came from wealthy families who could afford to keep them locked up here until they died."

"What about that chapel?" I said, pointing at a building on the far side of the cemetery. Its old walls were covered with ivy, cracks ran across the windows and the roof was in bad shape. The chapel was a depressing sight, made worse by the rain pounding down from the black sky. "Was it part of the asylum?"

"Probably, but I don't know for sure. The door has been locked for many years, so I've never been inside."

Just before we turned away, something dreadful happened. A raven swept down out of the stormy skies, spread its wings, and landed on a rusty weather vane above the chapel door. There was a tremor in my voice when I spoke to Jayne.

"Are you superstitious?"

"No, Liz, I'm not. Why do you ask?"

"Something awful is going to happen in the chapel, Jayne. That bird resting on the weather vane is the worst kind of omen."

"Your family must find your superstitions maddening, Liz," Jayne said. Her smile remained on her face as we left the room and started climbing an oak staircase, which spiralled up to the next floor, but on that staircase the smile disappeared. I never saw it again.

Jayne's mood changed just after we passed the gnome coming down the staircase. I call him the gnome because he resembled those little statues you see in people's gardens, except of course this guy was alive. He was very tiny and very old, with a little wrinkled brown face like an old apple that's been lying around a long time. Horribly, his face was exactly like the evil brass knocker I'd seen on the front door. He was smoking a miniature pipe as he came down the stairs, and he looked at me with tiny eyes that sparkled. "A stranger! May you stay with us long, and may you rest in peace."

I stared at him as he continued down the stairs, trailing smoke from the pipe. Then I turned to Jayne. "Why did he say *rest in peace*? That's what people write on tombstones."

"I'm sure Crouch meant no harm, Liz. He's been head gardener at Blackwater for a long, long time."

"Since the days of the lunatic asylum?"

"Of course not," Jayne said, sounding annoyed. "I know what you're thinking, and it's not polite."

We continued up the spiral staircase in silence.

The next hallway seemed darker, perhaps because it was panelled in old wood. The only light came from small bulbs that glowed above oil portraits on the walls. Jayne stopped at a portrait of a man whose face looked like a sad bloodhound. "That was the Baron's father," she said, then led me to a door at the end of the hallway.

"We'll only stay a few minutes. I'm worried about straining the Baron."

As she opened the door, I was overwhelmed by the reek of garlic. I've never known a room to have bad breath, and I mentally held my nose as we walked in. Then I saw that the walls were covered with crucifixes, and wondered if someone was playing a joke on me, because two defences against vampires are garlic and crucifixes. When I noticed the mirrors hanging everywhere, I turned to Jayne. "What's going on?"

"When he was a boy in Romania," she said, watching me closely, "the Baron heard tales of vampires. Lately he has begun to believe that such creatures exist, and I cannot convince him otherwise. It is sad to watch a great man suffer foolishly."

I pointed to the mirrors. "Is that why ..."

"As I'm sure you know, Liz, it is said that a vampire will not cast a reflection in a mirror. Whenever the Baron receives a visitor, he first looks at that person's reflection. The doctors, his lawyer, even his poor fiancée, all must be examined in the looking glass. It will happen with you, too."

"Where is the Baron?"

"In his bedroom. Wait here, and I will fetch him."

Surprisingly, my nose quickly adjusted to the

garlic. My eyes went quickly around the large room, studying the Persian carpets, old carved cabinets and chairs, oil paintings in gold frames, and the massive fireplace where logs burned cheerfully, throwing light into a room that was otherwise very dark. Outside the leaded-glass windows the storm continued.

"Good afternoon."

The voice made me jump. Turning, I saw a man in a wheelchair. I knew immediately that he was Baron Nicolai Zaba, the creator of a vast pulp and paper empire and one of Canada's wealthiest people, not simply because I'd seen his face in magazines, but because of the dignity and authority I sensed. His hair was thick and grey and he had penetrating eyes of the most unusual blue, exactly like a Siamese cat. As I walked toward the Baron those eyes flicked to the wall behind me, and I knew he was watching for my reflection.

"My dear girl," he said, and kissed my hand. "It's an honour to meet you. I am forever in your debt for saving my sweet Dionne's life. How can I ever thank you?"

"That's not necessary, sir. I was glad to help, and you were really kind to arrange for the ballet tickets. It's a real thrill to be invited to Blackwater."

"Your visit was actually suggested by Lobos, but I was happy to agree." Turning in his wheelchair, he looked into the bedroom. "Here he comes now."

I'd forgotten about the Baron having a valet named Lobos. Then, as the man emerged from the shadows of the bedroom, I remembered how he'd been described by Simon Sharples.

Weird.

It was the perfect word for Lobos. He was short

and plump, with a body like an egg and a face like mashed potatoes. All lumpy, if you know what I mean, and on the pale side of white. His eyes bulged from his face, and they were bloodshot. Taking a not-too-clean handkerchief from his pocket, he rubbed at his nose, which was red and runny, and then limped forward to shake my hand.

"Welcome to Blackwater, Liz Austen."

7

Lobos stared at me through glassy eyes, and his voice quavered, like it was coming through water. When I shook his soft hand, I felt like running off in search of a bottle of disinfectant. I know all this sounds mean, but this guy really gave me a first class case of the creeps. As a matter of fact, the whole visit to Blackwater didn't seem like such a terrific idea anymore, what with its spooky chapel and cemetery. And I was beginning to wonder whether it was just a coincidence that practically everyone I'd met so far in Ottawa was interested in vampires.

Jayne came from the bedroom, looking worried, to stand beside the wheelchair. "Shouldn't you return to bed, Baron? I'm anxious about your health."

"Perhaps you're right." Baron Zaba looked around the room, like he was searching for vampires in the dark corners, and then he crossed himself. Firelight glinted from a gold crucifix at his throat. "Will you join me for the evening meal, dear girl?"

"I'd love to, sir."

"Good." Looking weary, the Baron turned to Lobos. "I will rest now."

"Certainly, Baron."

They disappeared into the bedroom, and I left the suite with Jayne. In the hallway I turned to her with a smile. "Baron Zaba is really nice, and so handsome. Speaking of which, when do I meet your hubby?"

"You just did. I'm married to Lobos."

I was so stunned that my mouth dropped open. Then I realized I was being rude and slammed it shut. But, really, I just couldn't imagine *anyone* marrying Lobos. "Oh," I mumbled. "He, uh, he's got, um, a great sense of humour."

I felt like a total idiot, but Jayne didn't even seem to notice. Her eyes stared into space, and she signed deeply as we walked down the hallway. From somewhere above us came a rattling sound that was probably thunder, but made me wonder if there was a monster chained to a wall in the attic. That's how edgy I was feeling.

My mood improved when we reached the kitchen and I saw Orli. We gave each other a big hug, then Orli introduced me to her mother. Mrs. Yurko had a sweet face, with eyes the colour of

the sky, and a round body that showed how
much she loved to cook. When we were introduced, I discovered that she didn't speak much
English.

"*Uscatele*," she said, handing me some pastry.
"Eat, is good!"

Orli smiled. "Those are called rabbit ears, Liz.
A favourite dessert in Romania."

As I chewed some of the pastry, I watched Mrs.
Yurko stir a pot on the stove. "I'm eating with
the Baron tonight, Orli. Will we be having
Romanian food?"

"For sure. My mother has been brought to
Canada for that reason. The Baron wants to eat
only the foods of his youth, in hopes of improve-
ments in his health. The heart of the Baron is not
well."

Even though Jayne had left the kitchen, I
leaned close to Orli. "That valet, Lobos, is something else," I whispered. "Don't you love his red
eyes and runny nose?"

"He has, I think, an allergy to animals."

"I haven't noticed any pets around here."

Orli shrugged. "I am told to not have a cat
here. Which is sad, because in Cluj I had many.
Such lovely cats, and all left behind in
Romania."

At this moment, Mrs. Yurko happened to
glance at Orli and a look of fear crossed her face.
Then she let fly in Romanian, speaking incredi-
bly quickly and gesturing with the wooden
spoon she held. When it was all over, the poor
woman began to cry, and Orli went to comfort
her.

"What's wrong?" I asked. "Is it something I
said?"

Orli shook her head. "My mother is upset for a
week now, maybe two. It is difficult on me, trying

to understand. Just now she saw my left eye twitching, as I speak to you of cats, and she says that means we will receive bad news. I am telling her, over and over, do not be supersititous but she is old Romanian, and believes in such things as the evil eye."

"What does she think about Dracula?"

Mrs. Yurko stared at me with her bright blue eyes, then spoke rapidly in Romanian. The only word that made sense was *Dracul*, but I certainly understood the fear on her face.

"What's wrong, Orli? What have I said?"

"In Romania, my uncle has a serious illness. The village people are teasing him, saying he is Dracula, because of his face. This makes my mother sad."

"Oh, Orli, I'm so sorry." I went forward to Mrs. Yurko, and hugged her round body. "Please tell your mom I apologize." As the two of them exchanged more words in Romanian I continued to hug the woman, but when I let go there was still dread and despair on her face.

What a place Blackwater was turning out to be! Nobody seemed happy, not even Orli, who had a faraway look in her eyes as she accompanied me to the burgundy room, where I unpacked my suitcase. I tried to find out what was troubling her, but without any luck, so I was feeling pretty glum when I went to the Baron's suite for the evening meal.

Once again I was overwhelmed by the smell of the garlic that hung in bunches around the windows. The Baron was waiting in his wheelchair, wearing a silk dressing gown. Lobos hovered nearby. Jayne sat in a corner of the room, wearing a red dress that suited her dark hair and eyes, but her mouth was tight and pinched, and her eyes looked worried.

"Good evening, everyone!" I said, trying to sound cheerful. "I could eat a horse!"

Lobos wiped his nose with his hanky. "You may have to settle for jellied pork hocks."

The Baron had been studying me in a mirror. Now he wheeled around, smiling. "Lobos refers to *racituri*, one of my favourite dishes, but in your honour I have asked Mrs. Yurko to prepare *sarmale* and *cirosti*."

"Sounds great!" I said, though I didn't have a clue what he meant. "How are you feeling tonight, Baron Zaba?"

"Not very well, my dear."

Lobos went to the door. "With your permission, sir, I'll go to the kitchen for the food."

"Why not let Mrs. Yurko bring it up?"

"She's not feeling well. I thought I'd try to help."

"Very kind of you, Lobos."

The meal, which turned out to be cabbage rolls and a dough filled with cheese, was good but too salty for my taste. The Baron didn't eat much. He answered my questions about Romania politely, but with few words, and spent a lot of time touching the crucifix at his neck, or crossing himself. During the meal, which we ate at a large oak table, Jayne seemed lost in thought, so only Lobos and I talked. I found myself liking the guy because he asked a lot of questions about Winnipeg, and made some really funny remarks. Jayne was right. He really did have a terrific sense of humour.

When we'd finished nibbling rabbit ears for dessert, the Baron handed me a crucifix. "Keep this with you tonight, dear girl, and remember to lock your windows and door."

Jayne shook her head. "Really, Baron Zaba, I

must protest. I know how you feel about vampires, but —"

"She is a guest in my home. It would be terrible if she came to harm."

"Baron, you must believe me. Vampires do not threaten Blackwater."

The Baron glanced at Jayne with those Siamese-cat eyes, and I knew he did not believe her. Then he looked at me. "According to Lobos, you share my feelings about the undead of Transylvania. Tomorrow, let us discuss these things." Before I could agree, he added, "If tomorrow comes."

I stood up from the table, clutching my crucifix. Suddenly I felt cold all over. "I think I'll go to my room now. Thanks for your hospitality, Baron Zaba."

He smiled at me sadly. "If you say your prayers tonight, dear girl, pray for my soul."

Jayne pushed back her chair. "I'll walk Liz to her room."

"I can find my way, Jayne."

"I'm sure you can, but I insist."

Jayne took me by the elbow and practically shoved me out of the room. Once we were in the hallway, she turned to me. "Why don't you give me that crucifix, Liz? You won't be needing it."

"Maybe you're right." I attempted a laugh, but failed. "All I know is, I'll sleep just a little bit better with it beside me on the pillow."

"I hope you won't encourage the Baron's feelings about vampires. He gets so wound up that I'm afraid for his heart. When he asks you about the subject tomorrow, please don't discuss it."

To reach my room, we had to climb some stairs at the back of the house. They were really dark, because of the wood panelling, so I missed my footing as we climbed and fell forward. When Jayne helped me up, I looked at my hand.

"I've cut myself."

As Jayne looked at the blood on my hand a strange feeling passed over me. *I've been here*, I thought. *This has happened before.* For a second I knew what Jayne would do next.

"Lick the wound," she said. "That will clean it."

The blood was salty on my tongue, which made me realize how thirsty I'd been since eating. As we continued up the stairs I heard the wind whistling past the house, and the rumble of thunder.

"This is better than a prairie storm," I said, trying to forget how nervous I felt. "Ours don't last so long."

"I've never known the weather to be so ugly. It's really quite frightening."

When I had first seen my room during the day, it had seemed really pretty. There was a small tiled fireplace, a mahogany bureau with a silver brush set, some satin-upholstered chairs trimmed with lace, and a fantastic four-poster bed covered with a cosy eiderdown and fat pillows.

Now, however, I felt differently.

Instead of looking cheerful, the room was gloomy. The dark-red wallpaper was stained where people with greasy hair had leaned against it while sitting in chairs. Above the bed was a portrait of a peasant whose eyes, I now noticed, looked haunted by fear. Branches tapped against the window, and the wind rattled the glass.

But the worst of all were the roses. They hadn't been in the room earlier, I knew that. I reached out to touch the petals to see if they were real, then turned to Jayne. "These roses are such a strange colour. Pale purple. It's like someone sucked the blood out of them. Where could they have come from, Jayne?"

"Probably a gift from Crouch."

"The gardener?"

"Yes."

I shivered, remembering his eyes, the miniature pipe he'd been smoking as we passed on the staircase, and his words: *May you rest in peace.* "I don't want these roses in my room, Jayne. Please, can you take them away?"

"Certainly, Liz." She picked them up. "Why don't I also take that crucifix?"

"No way," I said, shaking my head. "Not a chance. Never. No, no, no."

"You're a stubborn girl." She kissed my cheek with cool lips. "I'll see you in the morning."

"Okay," I said. Then I remembered the Baron's last words: *If tomorrow comes.*

When Jayne was gone I carefully locked the door and put the key in my skirt pocket. Then I looked around, wondering why Jayne had picked this room for me to sleep in. Someone had put a pitcher of water and a glass on the bureau, which was a real gift because I was feeling so thirsty from the salty *sarmale* and *cirosti*. I gulped down a glassful, then had a second after getting into my pyjamas. I knew it was bad luck to sleep in a bed that faces north, but I had no idea which direction north might be so I didn't move the bed. I got under the covers and switched out the light.

I've never experienced satin sheets before, so that was a treat. But the mattress was too soft. I felt suffocated with the window closed, and my head was strangely fuzzy. I tossed and turned, then got up for more water. As I sipped it, my eyes watched the rain splattering against the window.

Just before getting back into bed, I looked at the peasant. Her eyes seemed to be watching me. Feeling a bit silly, I took the portrait down and leaned it against the wall. Then once again I cuddled down into the satin sheets and tried to sleep.

I saw graves in an old cemetery. Bodies rose out of the graves, and I knew they were the people who had lived at Blackwater when it was an insane asylum. With a gasp I sat up in bed. Had I been dreaming? No, it was more like a vision. I shook my head, trying to clear it of fog, and lay down again.

Now I saw beautiful shapes and designs playing inside my head. I smiled, feeling happy, and listen to the music from Swan Lake. What a lovely way to fall asleep! The music swirled and danced. Out of the lake came the prince, smiling. Then he disappeared and I heard a *tap-tap-tap* sound.

I turned my face to the door, where the tapping came from, and saw that it was slowly opening. It was hard to focus my eyes, but I still watched as a hand appeared around the door. As lightning filled the room with a burst of white light, I saw that the fingernails were sharp, and hair sprouted from the palm of the hand.

Next I saw a face. It wasn't the face of a man, but rather a creature shaped like a man. Hair grew thick on his head, and his teeth were sharp and pointed, but those things I hardly noticed. Instead I was only aware of his skin, which glowed.

The creature stepped into the room, but I could do nothing but stare at him in terror. My limbs felt heavy, and the soft mattress seemed to hug me like a straitjacket. The flashes of lightning were almost constant as the creature came toward me, filling the room with his foul breath.

I opened my mouth to scream, but no sound came out. The crucifix! I wanted to reach for it, but my hand wouldn't move. Desperately I tried to squirm away from the creature, but nothing happened. I was unable to move as he reached the bed and stood over me, his glowing eyes fixed on mine and his teeth glistening in the terrible bursts of white light from the storm outside. Again I tried to scream, and again, while I smelled the creature's rank breath and waited for the teeth to plunge into my neck.

But it didn't happen. Suddenly there was a loud noise from the hallway. The creature whirled around, and within a second was gone from the room. For a few minutes I cried, and tried without success to get out of the bed. Then my head was filled with visions of Swan Lake. The music was sweet, and soon I slept.

8

In the morning, sunshine filled my room.

"It couldn't have happened," I whispered to
myself. "That creature was just a nightmare."
Slowly I crawled out of bed and went to the
window. Every muscle in my body ached, but my
head felt as clear as the blue skies above. Gusts
of wind bent the branches of the trees and tossed
the flowers in the beautiful gardens. At the dis-
tant fountain, I could see water being blown
away from the mouth of the sea serpent.

Then I saw Crouch.

He was kneeling beside a flower bed with a trowel in his hand and that miniature pipe in his teeth. His eyes looked straight into mine. With a gasp I stepped back from the window and pulled the curtains shut. My body was trembling, and I had to sit on the bed until I got my nerves under control. Then I tried to pour myself a glass of water, but the pitcher was so full that it slopped onto the bureau and I trembled again. "It was a nightmare," I kept telling myself. "Just believe that, and you'll be fine."

I was in such bad shape that I put on my right shoe first. That's as unlucky as passing someone on the stairs, and I shuddered when I remembered passing Crouch yesterday on the spiral staircase. Then I put my hand in my pocket, and touched the key to my bedroom door.

"Wait a minute," I whispered to myself. "*Wait a minute!*"

I clearly remembered locking my bedroom door last night. If it was still locked now, then I had proof that the creature had been a nightmare. I went quickly to it and turned the handle.

The door opened.

"Oh no," I said, feeling tears in my eyes. "That means he was real!" I collapsed onto the bed, and was staring at the ceiling when Jayne entered the room.

"Good morning, sleepyhead! It's almost noon, and everyone's wondering where you are."

"Jayne, something terrible happened last night." I gave her all the details, ending with my discovery of the key in my pocket. "I know I locked the door."

"A vampire in here last night? Liz, that's impossible."

"But I *saw* him with my own eyes!"

Jayne shook her head, but I could tell she was upset. She went to the window, opened the curtains and stood looking at Crouch, then turned to me.

"Now, Liz," she said, pretending to be cheerful, "how about some breakfast? Orli is waiting for you in the kitchen."

"May I see the Baron first? I want to tell him about the vampire."

Jayne sat down beside me on the bed. "Liz, listen to me. The Baron has a weak heart. All this talk of the undead is not good for him. He insists he is threatened by vampires, and I cannot convince him otherwise. If you tell him about your nightmare, it won't help."

"It wasn't a nightmare, Jayne! I saw that creature with my own eyes."

"I don't believe you."

That got me angry. I stomped out of my room, ran down the stairs, and was trying to decide how to find the kitchen when I saw Lobos coming out of the Baron's suite. "This is a surprise, Liz," he said, smiling. "I thought you'd be exploring the grounds on such a lovely day. Baron Zaba was just saying how much he enjoyed your company last night."

I was tempted to ask permission to see the Baron, but in my heart I knew that Jayne was right and that I mustn't upset him. I was turning away when Lobos put a soft hand on my arm. "Come and say good day to the Baron. He'd be very pleased."

"All right."

The smell of garlic seemed especially powerful. The Baron sat at the window in his wheelchair, staring down at the cemetery. He looked terrible when he turned around. His forehead was deeply creased, his eyes were dark and bleary, and he sighed while examining my reflection in a mirror. Then he shook his head.

"Dear girl, I feel I'm not long for this world. With poor Dionne so ill in hospital, and danger pressing in from every side, there is nothing to live for. Treasure youth while you can, for soon you will be old and tired." He crossed himself, then touched the gold crucifix at his throat. "Did you sleep in safety last night?"

I wanted to answer the Baron honestly, but I also didn't want to upset him further. Then Lobos smiled at me. "You can say whatever is on your mind, Liz. Baron Zaba is stronger than you may think."

The Baron rolled toward me in his wheelchair. "Something happened," he said anxiously. "Tell me the exact details."

I didn't have any choice. By the time I finished the Baron's face was white, and he was gasping for air. I thought he was having a heart attack, but Lobos massaged his back and spoke soothingly, which seemed to help. "Dear girl," the Baron said at last, "you must leave Blackwater at once. You are in great danger."

This shocked me, because I didn't want to leave. There was the boathouse to investigate, and I wanted to have a look at the chapel. Besides, I was beginning to have my doubts about the vampire myself. Maybe it *had* been just a nightmare.

Lobos looked at me. "Do you *want* to leave, Liz?"

"Not really."

He turned to Baron Zaba. "I think she will be safe here, sir. Certainly there will be no danger until sunset, because vampires prowl only by night, and perhaps Jayne will stay with Liz tonight for protection."

"She must leave at once!"

Lobos put a comforting hand on the Baron. "Let me discuss it with her." Leading me into the hallway, he closed the door of the suite. "I'm sure Jayne will keep watch with you tonight. I know you share the Baron's feelings about vampires, but I really believe these events can be explained."

"Well, it would be nice to stay."

"It's settled, then."

There was a movement in the hallway. We both turned to see Mrs. Yurko approaching with a tray of food. Overnight she seemed to have grown old. Her face sagged, the white hair which yesterday had been so carefully combed was now scraggly, and her eyes stared at us blankly as she entered the suite.

I was anxious to tell Orli about my experience, and also to find out what was troubling her mother, so I hurried through the long hallways toward the kitchen. But as I thought about Mrs. Yurko, I wondered about that tray of food she was taking to Baron Zaba. What if he lifted his tea cup and a black widow spider crawled out? Possibly the tea contained a potion that would paralyze the Baron, and allow a vampire to enter his bedroom to suck the blood from his neck. Or maybe someone had borrowed rat poison from the garden shed and injected it into the hard-boiled eggs.

I stopped walking, then shook off the idea. My imagination was getting the best of me.

Reaching the kitchen, I hugged Orli. Then I told her everything, including my suspicions about the food tray. "Maybe someone is tampering with the Baron's food. That stuff we had last night was really salty."

"The *sarmale* and *cirosti*? We also ate those, in

the kitchen, and found them excellent. Why harm Baron Zaba? It is not making sense."

"Maybe not making cents, but how about dollars?" Orli didn't get the play on words. "The Baron is a wealthy man, Orli. If he dies, who inherits this huge house and the antique furniture? Not to mention the pulp and paper empire, and that air-conditioned limousine, and tickets to the ballet. Figure out who inherits, and you've got your villain."

"Well, of course, once he is married, Dionne will be the heiress."

"Aha!" I said triumphantly. "And she's still in the hospital. I'm sure that man we saw swimming after her was trying to harm her."

Orli shook her head. "Liz, I must tell you this. I have my doubts."

"So does Jayne, but that isn't going to stop me. How about helping me do some investigating? I'd like to take a closer look at the boathouse."

"I was going to take you on a tour of the grounds today. Come, then. The boathouse is not far."

I expected to head straight for the boathouse, but when we got outside I saw the limousine glistening in the sunshine outside an enormous garage with room for 10 cars. "Orli, where does Simon Sharples live?"

"In the attic of the garage. He has an apartment, said to be quite pleasant."

"How about paying him a visit?" There was something peculiar about Simon. Why would such a good-looking guy waste his time being a chauffeur? Why did Simon seem to dislike Lobos and Jayne so much?

I'm not exactly sure what I had in mind, but it's often a good technique to surprise a person. Catch him off guard, and he might say something useful to your investigation. When there was no answer to our knocks on Simon's door, I turned the handle.

"Simon?" I called, stepping into the apartment. "It's Liz and Orli. May we talk to you?"

There was no reply. We were in a large room with white walls and big windows that let in cheerful splashes of sunlight. A yellow curtain billowed at an open window and there were bright rugs scattered around the polished floor. On the walls were travel posters from countries like France and Spain. "He's a real reader," I said to Orli. "Look at all the books and magazines."

"We'd better go, Liz."

"You're right." Then, as we turned to leave, Orli looked at a picture on the door.

"Who are these people, I wonder? Such solemn faces."

"It's a high school grad picture. Let's find Simon."

That wasn't hard to do, because his handsome face jumped right out of the picture. But what interested me more was the person standing next to him. "Hey, I think I recognize her!"

"That's the Baron's fiancée," Orli said.

"Why is she in the picture with Simon?"

"They went to school together. As a matter of fact, it was Simon who introduced Dionne to the Baron. It was at a staff party."

I wanted to study the photo more closely, but Orli pulled me out of the room.

A few minutes later we were heading toward the cemetery. It didn't bother me to walk among the tombstones with the warm sun on us, but it took courage to approach the chapel. I'd felt nervous about it since I'd seen the raven on the rusty weather vane.

"I wonder," said Orli. "What can it be like inside?"

"All cobwebs and thick dust, and mice nibbling the prayer books. But Jayne told me the chapel is locked." We approached the building along a cinder path that was thick with weeds and tall grass. The chapel door was of heavy wood, black with age and covered with ivy growing wild. I looked at the rusty door handle and the keyhole, which was designed for a huge, old-fashioned key.

"Hey!" I exclaimed, kneeling down. "Look at this, Orli."

"What? I see nothing."

"Look how the rust has been scratched. You can see the metal shining through. Someone's used a key on this recently." I turned the handle and pushed. To my surprise, the chapel door creaked open. A smell of must and dirt came to our noses.

"I wonder who unlocked this place?" I stepped cautiously inside, thinking the floor might collapse. The air was dark and seemed to be full of dust. Sunlight struggled inside through filthy windows, sending feeble shafts of light down to touch the altar and the wooden pews.

"It's lonely in here," Orli said. "I think ..."

"Listen!" I held up a warning hand and turned to look out the door. I'd heard the sound of feet pushing through the long grass of the cemetery, and now someone came into sight.

Simon Sharples.

The chauffeur was frowning. At first I thought he would find us, and shrank back into the gloom, but then he disappeared around the corner of the chapel. I looked at Orli. Her eyes were huge.

"What does he want, Liz?"

"I don't know. We'd better find out."

I waited a few minutes in case Simon was circling the chapel and might catch us coming out the door. Then I grabbed Orli's arm and we hurried outside. I pulled the door closed, wishing it wouldn't creak so loudly, and then went to the corner of the chapel where I'd last seen Simon.

"I wonder where he has gone?" Orli said.

"That grass tells us." I pointed to the trail of crushed tall stems that Simon had left behind. "He must have gone into those woods on the far side of the cemetery. Let's try to find him."

There was no sign of Simon when we reached the woods. My heart thumped uncomfortably when I thought of hidden eyes watching. I knelt down to study the ground.

"I think he went in that direction," I said, pointing.

"How do you know?"

"There are dead leaves everywhere, dry on top. But some of them, leading to those silver birches, are wet. His feet kicked up the leaves as he walked, and they landed upside down." We followed the trail to the silver birches, then discovered a rocky hill sloping down toward more trees. Through the leaves I could see the sparkle of the river, but there was no sign of Simon.

"He went that way," Orli said, pointing at a part of the hill where moss had been torn away by Simon's feet. "You notice, Liz, I am learning from you."

At the bottom of the hill we lost the trail until I noticed a branch that had just been broken. We managed to find another shortly after, and then a trail of overturned leaves combined with broken moss, so we were feeling pretty proud of our detective abilities when we reached the riverbank.

"Isn't that the boathouse?" I asked, pointing at a white structure some distance along the bank. "I wonder if Simon's heading there?"

We never found out. Suddenly a tall figure jumped out from behind some trees and we both screamed.

Simon stood before us, looking furious. "Are you following me?" he demanded in a voice that was frightening because it was so quiet.

"Um," I said, "we, uh, we ..."

"Answer me!"

"I guess, well, I suppose you'd call it following. We were just curious, Simon. Honest."

"You've no right to invade my privacy. I'm going to tell Baron Zaba about this lamentable behaviour by a person who's his guest. As for you, Orli, I'm shocked that you would spy on me. Your mother certainly wouldn't approve."

"Please, Simon, do not be angry. This would not be called spying."

"What would you call it?"

Orli shrugged, keeping her eyes on the ground. I felt badly that I'd led her into this mess. "Please, Simon," I said. "Don't blame Orli, and don't tell her mother. It's all my fault. I was just curious, that's all."

Simon studied me. His eyes were narrow, and his gorgeous face was red with hostility. "Curiosity killed the cat," he said. "Remember that, young lady." Turning, he pushed aside some bushes and disappeared into the woods.

9

I watched Simon crash off angrily through the
bushes. Why was he so touchy? What was he
trying to hide? I turned to Orli.

"Listen, can we walk to the boathouse?"

"I suppose so. After we have been there, we
can take the road up the hill. It leads directly
from the boathouse to the big mansion."

"I wonder why Simon didn't use that road?
Why come through the woods?"

"It defeats me. I cannot think of one reason."

It was difficult to reach the boathouse. We had to jump between big rocks along the riverbank, and sometimes swing around trees that hung over the water, so we were both sweating by the time we stepped onto the dock.

Inside the boathouse, several canoes were stacked along the wall. It was hard to see much else, because the only light came from the door behind us, but the smell of fuel was powerful, and I thought I could see a couple of outboard engines attached to wooden supports.

With Orli behind me, I walked across the boathouse floor to stairs that led up to a closed door.

"There's a room or something up there," I whispered to Orli. "That's where I saw the face in the window. I'm sure it was the man who chased the Baron's fiancée in the river."

"What do you plan?"

"Let's go up and look around. If someone's there, we can pretend we're selling magazine subscriptions or something."

Even though I had Orli for company, my heart was making a wild noise as we started to climb the stairs. It was so dark, with just a bit of daylight seeping in from the outside. Just as we reached the top, I felt something soft brush against my legs.

Looking down, I saw a large cat.

"She is a beauty!" Orli whispered, bending down to stroke the cat. It rubbed against Orli, wrapping its luxurious tail around her arm, and filling the air with a loud purr. "This is a Persian. How strange is the smell of lavender in her fur."

I picked up the cat and took a good sniff. "Smells like perfume. It really is strong."

Sitting down on the stairs, Orli put the cat in her lap. "It brings back a memory of visiting in childhood the village of my aunt and uncle."

"The cat?"

"No, the smell. I remember my aunt was painting eggs in the Romanian tradition. The kitchen was full of sunshine. It is sad she is now dead."

I'd almost forgotten why we'd come to the boathouse. I put my ear to the door and listened for sounds, then knocked. When there was no reply, I tried again. Nothing. Cautiously I tried the door. It was locked.

"Let's get out of here, Orli. This place is bad luck. There's something going on, but I can't get a handle on it. This boathouse spooks me."

"She is a lovely kitty," Orli said, rubbing her face against the cat. "I may come to visit again, you little sweetie."

Curiosity killed the cat. Both Jayne and Simon had made it sound like a warning. As I watched Orli giving the cat one last pat, I wondered what a friendly Persian was doing in the boathouse. They were expensive cats, and this one looked well groomed and well fed.

It felt good to be back in the sunshine. I didn't even mind that my investigation of the boathouse had been a flop. Then, as we started up the road toward the mansion, I was surprised to see Jayne coming our way. She looked ready to explode.

"What are you two doing here?" she exclaimed.

"Just having a look around," I said. "Isn't it a lovely day?"

Jayne didn't answer. Her eyes were fixed on the boathouse and a nerve twitched in her cheek. I could have sworn that several white hairs had appeared on her head overnight. "Liz, I'd like to talk to you about what happened last night in your room."

"Fire away."

"I have to do a small errand first. Would you mind waiting at the house for me?"

"Sure."

"Orli knows where I live. The door's unlocked. I'll meet you there in half an hour."

I watched her continue down the hill to the boathouse, wondering if we should follow. But she stopped on the dock and stood watching, obviously waiting for us to leave, so we turned and climbed the hill.

"Does Jayne have her own house?" I asked Orli.

"No," she said, breathing heavily because of the steep climb. "She is in the attic. I shall die of heart attack climbing way up there!"

I was also gasping for air. "No wonder the doctors make Baron Zaba stay put in his suite. Getting around Blackwater Estate is murder."

By the time we reached the attic, Orli and I were ready for the cardiac ward. We leaned against the wall, sucking air into our lungs, and then finally opened Jayne's door. It was very pleasant inside, with thick shag carpeting, some lovely teak furniture, and even a small fireplace. On the mantelpiece was a picture of a nice-looking woman with white hair. Beside the picture was a large pile of lottery tickets.

"Someone's spent a lot of money on these," I said, flipping through the tickets. "Did you know that you've got a better chance of being struck by lightning than actually winning one of these things?" When Orli didn't answer, I turned around. She was staring at a man who stood in the bedroom door.

Lobos.

His mouth hung open, and his eyes bulged more than usual. He looked surprised and almost ... guilty. For a second I thought he had broken into Jayne's place. Then I realized that he was Jayne's husband, and that it was his apartment, too.

The shocked expression on Lobos' face disappeared quickly. Throwing down the blue-stained towel he'd been using to dry his hands, he came forward with a welcoming smile on his face. "Thank goodness you are here, Liz! I was wondering where to find you."

"You were looking for me? What for?"

Lobos took my arm and led me into the other room. "Look at that," he said, pointing at the wall, where someone had used chalk to write IN EVIL MEMORY. "Will you help me, Liz?"

"What do you mean?"

"Jayne has told me that you're a very observant girl, and that you've even investigated some crimes. I believe Simon Sharples wrote those words, but I need your help to get proof."

"Simon? Why him?"

"That man has never liked me. I suspect he's jealous of my closeness to the Baron and because I was the one who married Jayne." Lobos wiped his red eyes with a hanky. "Simon has been acting very strangely lately. I think he's planning something, and I'm afraid it may hurt Jayne or the Baron."

I stared at the words. *In evil memory.* They were a twisted version of what people put on tombstones, and I'd just seen Simon in the cemetery. I was about to mention this when Lobos went to the window.

"There's the cemetery," he said, almost as if he could read my mind. "I've seen Simon go into the chapel, so this morning I went to investigate. In the crypt I found the same words on the wall, written with the same blue chalk."

My scalp tingled, remembering the raven on the weather vane. "What's the crypt?"

"It's like a cellar underneath the chapel."

"How can I help?"

Lobos looked thoughtful. "I have a plan, but I need a brave person to be at my side. Will you come with me now to the chapel?"

"I don't know." I studied the man's pudgy face. I was anxious to explore the chapel myself. But could I trust Lobos? "Okay," I said at last. "I'll go, but only if Orli comes along."

"Fine," Lobos said. "Let's go ask her." He went through the door into the other room where Orli was waiting, but I paused to look around the bedroom, looking for something that would tell me about his personality. There were pictures on the walls, but the only interesting one showed Lobos and Jayne on their wedding day. The photographer had done a good job, making Lobos look almost human, and Jayne was lovely in her white dress with delicate flowers in her dark hair. On the bureau was a pile of loose change, a wallet, and the small plastic figure of a Mountie on horseback. Everything looked perfectly ordinary.

But I still didn't know if he could be trusted. *Weird.* That's what Simon had called him.

Minutes later we were outside the house. "What about Jayne?" Orli said. "She wanted to talk to you."

I snapped my fingers. "I forgot. Well, there's no sign of her, so we can come back later."

As we started walking toward the chapel, Orli looked at her watch. "I do not have much time, Lobos. I'll be late for work. I'm on the evening shift this week."

Lobos was breathing heavily, stopping every so often to wipe his red eyes and nose. "I'm trying," he said, "but this allergy of mine makes it difficult for me to move quickly. Go ahead to the chapel. I'll meet you there."

Glad of the excuse, we quickened our pace. "You know," I said to Orli when we reached the cinder path leading to the chapel, "this cemetery is actually very pretty with the sun on the trees and tombstones. It's a shame that Crouch doesn't cut the grass, and maybe plant a few flowers."

"He has fear of the cemetery. He told me so in the kitchen one day while drinking his tea. I laughed and called him superstitious, but he said evil lives among the tombstones."

"If he wants to see evil he should look in the mirror," I said, remembering that wrinkled face. *Rest in peace* he'd said on the spiral staircase, as the smoke from his pipe swirled around his head. Now someone had written *In evil memory* on Lobos and Jayne's wall.

We entered the chapel and leaned against a couple of pews while we waited for Lobos. "The air smells so dank and musty," I said. "I guess because the chapel's been closed up for so long." Finally, Lobos came in the door.

"I'm sorry to keep you waiting," he said.

Orli looked at her watch. "I cannot wait longer. I must go back to the house to change for work."

"That's okay, Orli," I said, waving. "I'll see you later."

As we watched Orli heading down the path leading to the big house, Lobos suddenly snapped his fingers. "Please wait here, Liz, and I'll be right back. I want to give Orli a message for her mother."

"Okay."

I didn't mind the idea of being alone in the

chapel until I actually was alone. Then it hit me, and I felt panic bubble up in my throat. I almost ran after them, but I didn't want to look like a chicken. After all, I thought, surely Liz Austen the Great Detective has enough courage to be alone for a few minutes in a chapel, even if it's dusty with age and smells like a grave.

Then I decided I even had enough courage to look around. Cautiously I went up the aisle, studying the stained-glass window above the altar. The blues and reds had a richness I'd never seen before, and I was interested in the Latin words written in old-fashioned script. For a minute I forgot the gloomy surroundings as I tried to work out the meaning of the words. Then I heard the scamper of little feet and turned to see a mouse dashing along the back of a wooden pew. It scrambled down to the floor and headed for an open door. Through the door I could see stone stairs leading down into darkness, and wondered if they led to the crypt. Somewhere down below, in the cellar of the chapel, were the blue-chalk words: *In evil memory*.

I walked toward the stairs. I figured I'd just take a peek at the crypt and then come straight back upstairs. No harm in that, if I could find enough inner strength to get down those stairs.

Curiosity killed the cat.

The stone walls of the stairwell were so cold and damp that moisture trickled down, gleaming in the faint light coming from above in the chapel. I narrowed my eyes, trying to see, afraid of tripping or maybe stepping on the mouse.

At the bottom of the stairs another door stood open. The air was thick with the odour of decay. I stepped through the doorway, promising myself that I would take only a quick look.

Then I saw it.

An open coffin.

It stood in the middle of the crypt. Enough light came from the doorway to show that it was black, with handles that looked like gold or brass, and was lined with white silk. It was on a small platform. My heart was thundering and my body had turned cold.

I knew what must be in the coffin, and I knew I should run. But I couldn't. Feeling almost hypnotized, I walked slowly forward across the dirt floor, stumbling on bits of rock, hearing the gasps of my breathing echo from the stone walls. Reaching the platform, I climbed its three wooden stairs and looked down at the coffin.

Inside lay the vampire. I had known he would be there, waiting for me, and yet I hadn't believed it possible. I looked down at the glowing skin, the sharp teeth and the hair sprouting from the hands crossed on his chest. From him rose the terrible reek of his breath, mixed curiously with a sweet smell like violets. His eyes were closed, but he wasn't dead. His chest rose and fell with the deep breathing of sleep, the sleep which comes between nights of roaming the countryside in search of victims.

What was I doing here? Suddenly I knew I was being a fool, and turned to flee. I jumped down from the platform, and was running toward the door which led to the stairs and freedom when I heard a creaking sound. Then, with horrified eyes, I watched the door slam shut.

10

"Let me out!" I screamed, pounding my fists on the door. "*Let me out!*"

Grabbing the handle, I pulled with all my strength. It refused to move. Again I screamed and slammed my hands against the wooden door until the flesh stung so much I had to stop. Tears ran down my face, and I dropped to my knees, moaning with horror.

"Please," I whispered, "please, open the door."

Twisting around, I stared into the black air,

fearing the approach of the vampire. A faint glow showed from somewhere in the distance, and I prayed that the vampire was still in the coffin. My scalp crawled with terror, and I thought my heart would explode as my eyes searched the darkness, waiting for the unspeakable horror to strike.

Then, to my surprise, I became calm. I tried to think clearly, to remember everything I had learned about vampires. I knew that vampires only roamed after dusk and that, for the time being, anyway, I was probably safe. I wrapped my arms around my shivering body, and leaned against the door with my eyes on the faint glow.

A long time passed, and I fell into a kind of sleep. Then I woke with a start. My body was now so cold that my teeth rattled, and I wondered if I would actually die in this terrible place. Remembering the lunatic asylum that had once been here, I pictured bodies buried behind the walls that surrounded me. Then I thought of rats. Were they waiting in the darkness, waiting to feast on my dead body?

"No," I moaned. "This can't be true. It's a nightmare. It must be."

I reached up, found the handle of the door, and pulled myself to my feet. Then, without thinking a miracle was really possible, I tried the door.

It opened. Stumbling forward, I found the stairs and ran up.

The chapel was in total darkness, and I realized that night had come to Blackwater. Was the vampire out of his coffin, and prowling the estate? I knew now that the Baron had been right to fear a vampire attack, and I knew I had to warn him.

I ran from the chapel. A splendid moon filled the sky, its silver light strong enough to outline every tombstone and every leaf of every tree. I gulped down some sweet-smelling air, then took off for the mansion. I knew Baron Zaba was in great danger.

Inside the house the hallways were empty. I took the stairs two at a time, then raced toward the Baron's suite. Reaching it, I knocked loudly and called his name. When there was no answer I started pounding, afraid that I was already too late.

"Who's there?" called a voice that sounded very old and very frightened.

"It's Liz!" I cried. "Liz Austen. You must open your door, Baron Zaba. I've got to tell you something."

Along the hallway, yellow lights glowed above the oil portraits of the Baron's relatives, and I realized that his father was staring at me with suspicious eyes. They seemed so real. It was almost like someone was hiding behind the portrait, watching me through holes cut in the canvas.

A bolt slid back in the door, then another, and finally a key turned in the lock. As the door opened I smelled garlic, and saw darkness. Someone sat in the wheelchair, but his face was too pale to recognize.

"Baron Zaba?" I said, trying not to sound frightened. "Is that you?"

His hand beckoned me inside. "Quickly," he whispered, "before it's too late."

As I stepped into the suite, he told me to bolt the door. Wheeling to the centre of the room, he turned to wait for me. Silver moonlight flooded in through the windows, shining on the man's face. I was relieved to see he really was Baron Zaba.

"Take this," the Baron said, handing me a

crucifix. "Then check the door to the tower, to be sure it's also locked."

"Where is it?"

"Through the bedroom. Quickly!"

The smell of garlic was even stronger in the bedroom. Huge bunches of it hung around both the windows and the door to the tower. I tried the handle several times, to be absolutely sure it was locked, then hurried back to Baron Zaba. His face turned ghastly as I told him what had happened in the crypt of the chapel.

"I will die tonight," he moaned. "I have known the fear of vampires since I was a little boy, listening to the tales in Romania." He crossed himself, then pressed a crucifix to his lips. Another was at his throat, shining in the moonlight that streamed through the windows. "When you came to the suite just now I wanted you to stay, to help stand guard against the vampire. But I know I am doomed. You must leave immediately."

"I can't do that."

"You must!"

I didn't know what to do. My story about the crypt had so upset the Baron that I was afraid he would have a heart attack at any second. How could I leave him alone? At the same time, he didn't want me to stay and neither did I. As I looked at him, trying to decide, the Baron glanced beyond me and his mouth dropped open. Then he lifted a trembling hand, moaned some words I couldn't understand, and collapsed.

Turning, I saw the vampire.

He stood in the bedroom door. His teeth gleamed in the moonlight, and his skin glowed. He raised his hands and started toward me, moving slowly, his eyes fixed on mine. I stepped backward, groaning, and stumbled against a chair. As I did, my eyes went to a mirror and I saw the vampire's reflection.

"You're real!" I said. "I can see you!"

A lamp stood on a nearby table. Reaching out, I switched it on. Warm yellow light filled the room. There was a gasp from the vampire, and I saw shock on his face as I held up the crucifix.

"Get back!" I shouted. "You don't scare me."

Again the vampire gasped. Then he turned and fled from the room. I knelt beside the Baron, afraid he'd had a heart attack. I called his name, and his eyes opened.

"It's okay, Baron Zaba! I saw his reflection. You're safe."

"My pills," he gasped. "Get them from my pocket."

I found a vial of pills in the Baron's dressing gown, shook one out, and handed it to him. With weak fingers he lifted it to his mouth. "I'll be all right, Liz." His voice was so faint that I had to lean close to hear. "Hand me the telephone. I'll phone Lobos and Jayne for help."

As soon as the phone was in his hand, I looked at the bedroom door. Was the vampire hiding in there, waiting to attack again? Quickly I went to the bedroom, where the tower door stood open. Hurrying to it, I saw spiral stairs. I followed them up to a small viewing platform under the moonlight. Far in the distance I could see the lights of Ottawa, but close at hand was only the darkness of the surrounding woods, and the silver path of the river.

A noise came from below. Leaning over the tower railing, I looked down. A door opened, and out stepped the vampire. I watched as he ran swiftly toward the cemetery. Then I headed for the tower stairs. Down and down I ran, twisting around and around those winding stairs, until I reached the door at the base of the tower.

Then I ran toward the cemetery. I paused when I reached the tombstones, searching for signs of the vampire. Suddenly he rose up from behind a tombstone and fled, looking like an enormous bat with his black cape streaming behind in the moonlight. As I started after him, my foot hit a large rock and down I went, sprawling on the hard ground.

By the time I stood up, the vampire had disappeared. I looked at the chapel, dark and threatening. Taking a deep breath, I ran across the cemetery. Pulling open the door to the chapel, I stepped inside.

For a moment I was surrounded by total darkness. When my eyes adjusted, I made out the dim shapes of pews and saw the altar. I took one step forward, then another, listening to the harsh sound of my breathing fill the chapel.

Finally I reached the stairs that led down to the crypt. For a long time I hesitated, trying to find courage, and then I heard the low murmur of voices coming from below.

I started down the stairs. The air was so black, I put out a hand to the wall to steady myself, then pulled it away when I felt the cold water that ran down the stone. At the same moment I stepped on something that felt like a rock. I stumbled, almost falling, and heard it bounce down the stairs, making a tremendous noise in the enclosed space.

The voices stopped speaking. Then I heard a woman cry out, "*Necuratul!*" A man shouted, "Silence!" After that I heard nothing but the slow dripping of water somewhere in the stairwell. Taking a deep breath, I continued down the stairs.

In the crypt the air was cold and damp. Darkness was everywhere, until a cigarette lighter suddenly flared up in the distance.

In its glow, I saw the terrified face of Orli's mother, Mrs. Yurko.

I called her name, and was walking toward her when I realized that someone else stood just behind her, with an arm twisted around her neck. Then the lighter shifted slightly, and I saw the twisted features of a vampire.

"Get back," the creature snarled, "or I'll bite her."

He bent his fangs toward Mrs. Yurko's neck. I stopped walking. Then I heard footsteps coming slowly down the stairs from the chapel, and turned to look. In the doorway was a familiar shape.

It was another vampire.

Slowly he advanced. Closer and closer he moved toward the glow of the cigarette lighter, which cast its yellow light on the twisted features of his face. I looked again at the vampire who held the lighter. In his hand was a silver-plated revolver.

"Get back!" he shouted. "If you come one step closer, I'll fire!"

The vampire kept walking.

"I warn you! *Get back!*"

Then Mrs. Yurko cried at the approaching vampire in a language I couldn't understand. She twisted away from the arm around her neck and her hand flew up, striking the revolver. With a flash and roar that were terrible, the gun went off. The cigarette lighter fell to the ground, plunging the crypt into darkness.

Seconds later two shapes filled the doorway as they escaped up the stairs to the chapel. Now I was alone with one other person, but who? The cigarette lighter flared into life, and I saw it was held by the vampire with the revolver.

He climbed onto the platform beside the coffin, holding the lighter high in the air. I knew he was searching for me. The yellow light flickered and flared, dancing on his evil eyes and sharp fangs, while I held my breath and prayed. The vampire slowly turned on the platform, his eyes searching the darkness. I knew he would soon find me.

Looking down at the dirt floor, I saw a rock. Swiftly I bent down, picked it up, and threw it across the crypt. As it smacked against the wall the vampire cried out and turned his revolver in that direction.

As he did, I ran the short distance to the platform, leapt on it, and knocked the vampire backwards. He fell into the coffin, shouting in horror. Slamming the lid down, I climbed onto the coffin. From inside I heard muffled cries, then felt the coffin lid shift as the vampire tried to force it open. Desperately I held on, knowing I had to keep the lid closed long enough for the oxygen inside to be used up. Then the vampire would pass out and I would be able to go for help.

As I clung to the coffin lid, I saw a beam of light from the direction of the stairs. Then a second beam, also from a flashlight, shone on the wet walls as two people came cautiously down.

"Help me!" I shouted. "Over here!"

"Are you safe, Liz?" It was Jayne.

"Yes. Who's that with you?"

"It's Simon. The Baron called us, and we've been looking everywhere for you."

I nearly collapsed with relief. Then I noticed that the pounding from inside the coffin had stopped. As Jayne and Simon approached, I got off the coffin to stand on the platform.

"There's some kind of vampire inside here."

"Let's take a look," Simon said. Opening the coffin, he shone his flashlight inside. "That's not a vampire. It's someone wearing a rubber mask. Let's get it off him."

As he reached for the mask, Jayne stopped him. "Let me do this," she said quietly.

Glancing at Jayne's face, I was surprised to see tears in her eyes. I couldn't understand why, but then she pulled off the vampire's mask and I saw the reason.

Lying inside the coffin was her husband, Lobos.

11

Four days later I found out why Lobos was in that coffin.

The details came out following the wedding of Baron Zaba and his fiancée, Dionne, in the chapel of a large Ottawa hospital. The Baron had been rushed to the hospital but had made a swift recovery from the shock of the vampire entering his suite. Dionne was also recovering in the same hospital, and the Baron didn't want the wedding postponed any longer.

My parents had given me special permission to stay in Ottawa for the ceremony. It was a thrill to be one of the guests. The bride and groom, both in wheelchairs, made a handsome couple. I was pleased when Dionne came to me after the ceremony with her thanks for what I'd done in the river.

"What happened, Dionne? Why were you in the river?"

"I was looking around the estate that day and happened to see the boathouse. I was curious, so I went inside and climbed the stairs. I had no idea anyone *lived* up there, so I opened the door. Standing inside was a ... vampire, holding a cat in his arms."

"A Persian," I said, glancing at Orli, who stood beside us. "We've met that cat."

"All I can remember," Dionne said, shuddering, "is that deformed face, and the cat purring in the creature's arms. He started to move toward me, and I ran down to the dock. I was so panicked, I leapt into the water and tried to swim for safety. I thought that ... creature ... was coming after me."

"Is that who followed you into the river?" I asked. "Was he the mystery man?"

"Actually, no, it wasn't ..." Dionne looked around uncomfortably as Jayne walked over to join our group.

"That's all right, Dionne," Jayne said. "I'll tell them what happened. I've had many long talks with my husband, and he's told me all the details of his plot against Baron Zaba."

For a long time Jayne was silent. Then she sighed. "I've been with Baron Zaba all my working life. A year ago Lobos was hired as valet. He seemed like such a fine man, with that marvellous sense of humour, so I was flattered when he asked me out. As time passed and I became fond of Lobos, I foolishly told him that I would inherit a large sum of money from the Baron on his death.

"Unknown to me, Lobos was a heavy gambler who owed a lot of money. I guess he decided to marry me, knowing I would eventually be worth a lot. But then Dionne and the Baron fell in love. Lobos feared that all the money would go to Dionne, so he decided to act fast. If the Baron could die before the marriage, I would still receive my inheritance."

Jayne looked at us with her sad eyes. "I don't believe that Lobos is an evil man. But he was greedy, and he had those gambling debts. He could never have murdered the Baron, but another plan had been brewing in his mind ever since Mrs. Yurko had arrived from Romania."

She looked across the room at Orli's mother, who was happily chatting to the Baron. "Lobos learned that Mrs. Yurko's brother suffered from a blood disease called porphyria, which gives its victims every appearance of being a vampire. The skin glows, the victim's teeth become prominent because the gums tighten, and thick hair grows all over the body.

"Lobos offered to fly Mrs. Yurko's brother to Canada, where treatment for porphyria is easily available. But as soon as the man arrived, Lobos started lying to Mrs. Yurko. He said that her brother was in the country illegally, and would be deported if the police found out. Not only that, but Mrs. Yurko and Orli would also be thrown out of Canada. Total lies, but she was terribly afraid. Now that Lobos had control over her, he made Mrs. Yurko agree to her brother acting the part of a vampire at the estate." Jayne looked at

Orli. "As you've found out, your mother had no idea why Lobos made this strange request.

"Your uncle was hidden in the boathouse. The poor man was wretchedly unhappy, so he was allowed to have a cat, despite Lobos' allergy. Then my husband set to work on Baron Zaba, playing on his boyhood fear of vampires, hinting that such creatures might exist at Blackwater Estate. He was softening up the Baron for another heart attack, one that would prove fatal. Then came the day you arrived at the boathouse, Dionne, and thought you saw a vampire. As you ran, screaming, to the river, Lobos was coming down the hill. He realized what had happened and swam after you, but was too late to stop you. Obviously he feared you would tell everyone about what you'd seen in the boathouse, but after your ordeal in the river, you were too deep in shock to do that."

"But why did you keep swimming from Lobos?" I asked. "I don't understand."

Dionne looked at Jayne almost apologetically before answering. "Simon and I have been friends for many years. As a matter of fact, he was the one who introduced me to the Baron. He had told me about his suspicions that Lobos was plotting against the Baron. I didn't believe him, of course. The Baron thought so highly of Lobos. But when I saw the angry look in Lobos' eyes when he followed me into the river, I knew that Simon had been right."

"No wonder Simon was so angry when Orli and I followed him through the woods the other day and ruined his plans," I said. "He was probably going to check out the boathouse. Lobos must have realized that Simon was getting close to the truth and tried to make him look guilty by writing IN EVIL MEMORY on the wall. If my eyes had been open a little wider, I'd have noticed that the words were written in blue chalk and that Lobos had left blue stains on the towel after washing his hands."

Jayne nodded. "You, Liz, were actually quite a big part of Lobos' plans. After hearing Orli describe how you felt about vampires, Lobos decided to have you invited to Blackwater so that you could see the creature and tell the Baron about it. Then the Baron would be completely convinced a vampire was roaming the estate, and would be really terrified.

"The night you arrived, Liz, Lobos went downstairs for the food. He added a lot of salt to your portion, which made you so thirsty that you drank several glasses of water from the pitcher that Lobos had put in your room. The water contained a powerful tranquillizer that made you unable to move when the vampire opened your door, using a key from Lobos, and pretended to attack. Later that night, while you slept, Lobos refilled your pitcher with ordinary water."

I held up the glass of ginger ale I'd been drinking. "I hope there isn't a mind-blaster in here!" I said, smiling. I gulped some down, then looked at Jayne. "Lobos lured me into the chapel by pretending he needed my help to investigate Simon. I guess he figured my curiosity would get me down to the crypt, where I'd see the vampire in the coffin." I shook my head and sighed. "If I hadn't been terrified out of my mind, I might have figured out right then that the creature in the coffin couldn't have been a vampire. Vampires only sleep in *closed* coffins."

Jayne nodded. "Then he locked you in the crypt until night, knowing you'd go straight to the Baron about what you'd seen. Shortly after, the vampire unlocked the suite's tower door to make his appearance. Baron Zaba might have had a fatal heart attack, Liz, if you hadn't seen the vampire's reflection in the mirror and told the Baron the creature couldn't be real."

"I chased the vampire into the cemetery, then lost him. When I went down to the crypt, Lobos was there in a rubber Dracula mask with Mrs. Yurko. How'd he get her to go down there?"

"By threatening to have her family thrown out of the country. I guess he hoped to use Mrs. Yurko as a hostage, if necessary, but she was saved when her brother returned to the crypt."

Orli studied Jayne's face. "Tell me, please. Did you not suspect your husband?"

"I confess that I did," Jayne replied. "But they say love is blind, and I guess it's true. It bothered me when Lobos asked me to question Liz at the ballet about her interest in vampires. Then she stayed at Blackwater overnight, and said a vampire almost attacked her. I told her she was wrong, that it couldn't have happened, because I refused to believe it was possible. Slowly, though, the evidence mounted up as I investigated."

As I sipped my drink, I thought back over the events at Blackwater. Then I snapped my fingers. "You know something else I completely missed, that linked the vampire and Lobos? It was his allergy to pets. His red eyes and runny nose must have been caused by visiting the boathouse where Mrs. Yurko's brother had the Persian cat. Remember, Orli, we smelled lavender in its fur? Later, when I saw the vampire in his coffin, I noticed the same smell. I guess I should have put all that together. Some detective I've been!"

As people laughed, Baron Zaba wheeled over to join our group. "You're all looking very cheerful!" he exclaimed, then noticed Jayne's sad face. "Except you, my dear, and for that I'm terribly sorry."

"It's not your fault I picked the wrong man, Baron Zaba."

"Jayne, I'm hoping that you will continue to work at Blackwater. I only wish Lobos had known that I never planned to take you out of my will. The inheritance will still be yours, since there is lots of other money to leave my dear wife."

"Thank you, Baron." Jayne shook her head. "Poor Lobos. He really did make a mess of things."

"He was a fine valet," the Baron said. "Fortunately, I have an excellent person to take his place. Mrs. Yurko's brother will be my new valet, once he has completed his treatment for porphyria."

"Great!" I exclaimed. "Will he be allowed to keep his cat?"

"Certainly. In addition, Orli, I invite you to have a cat of your own at Blackwater. They will cheer us all up."

"Cats are good luck to have around the house," I said. "It's especially good luck if a cat sneezes after the bride and groom return home from their honeymoon. But may I give you some advice, Baron and Mrs. Zaba? When you're on your honeymoon, try your best to see an elephant. Then your married life will be blessed with good fortune."

Baron Zaba laughed. "I'm going to phone the circus right now. When we leave this hospital, the biggest pachyderm in Ottawa will wave us bon voyage with its trunk."

Although it sounds strange, that's just what happened. But I'll save that story for another time!

Since Eric Wilson was born in Ottawa, it was a pleasure for him to return to his home town to research *Vampires of Ottawa*. Although Eric now lives in British Columbia, he is often "on the road" visiting schools to speak about his writing, or exploring various regions of Canada to discover settings for future books.

CODE RED AT THE SUPERMALL
A Tom and Liz Austen Mystery

Eric Wilson

They swam past gently-moving strands of sea-weed and pieces of jagged coral, then Tom almost choked in horror. A shark was coming straight at him, ready to strike.

Have you ever visited a shopping mall that has sharks and piranhas, a triple-loop rollercoaster, 22 waterslides, an Ice Palace, submarines, 828 stores, and a major mystery to solve? Soon after Tom and Liz Austen arrive at the West Edmonton Mall a bomber strikes and they must follow a trail that leads through the fabled spendours of the supermall to hidden danger.

THE GREEN GABLES DETECTIVES
A Liz Austen Mystery

Eric Wilson

I almost expected to see Anne signalling to Diana from her bedroom window as we climbed the slope towards Green Gables, then Makiko grabbed my arm. "Danger!"

Staring at the house, I saw a dim shape slip around a corner into hiding. "Who's there?" I called. "We see you!"

While visiting the famous farmhouse known as Green Gables, Liz Austen and her friends are swept up in baffling events that lead from an ancient cemetery to a haunted church, and then a heart-stopping showdown in a deserted lighthouse as fog swirls across Prince Edward Island. Be prepared for eerie events and unbearable suspense as you join the Green Gables detectives for a thrilling adventure.

SPIRIT IN THE RAINFOREST
A Tom and Liz Austen Mystery

Eric Wilson

The branches trembled, then something slipped away into the darkness of the forest. "That was Mosquito Joe!" Tom exclaimed.
  "Or his spirit," Liz said. "Let's get out of here."

The rainforest of British Columbia holds many secrets, but none stranger than those of Nearby Island. After hair-raising events during a Pacific storm, Tom and Liz Austen seek answers among the island's looming trees. Alarmed by the ghostly shape of the hermit Mosquito Joe, they look for shelter in a deserted school in the rainforest. Then, in the night, Tom and Liz hear a girl's voice crying *Beware! Beware!*

THE UNMASKING OF 'KSAN

Eric Wilson

Looking back, I saw Bear near the doorway.
I knew he'd never stop chasing us while Dawn had the
raven mask.
"Get rid of that thing!"
"Not a chance," she said. "Come on, run faster."

The theft of a valuable mask brings sorrow to Dawn's
people. Determined to recover it, she turns to Graham for
help and together they begin a search that plunges them
into suspense and danger. The rugged mountains and
surging rivers of northern British Columbia are the back-
drop to an adventure you will never forget.

SUMMER OF DISCOVERY

Eric Wilson

Rico's teeth were chattering so loudly that everyone could hear. Ian's breath came in deep gasps. A gust of wind slammed through the old building, shaking it so hard that every shutter rattled, and then they heard the terrible sound. Somewhere upstairs, a voice was sobbing.

Do ghosts of hymn-singing children haunt a cluster of abandoned buildings on the Saskatchewan prairie? The story of how the kids from Terry Fox Cabin answer that question will thrill you from page one of this exciting book. Eric Wilson, author of many fast-moving mysteries, presents here a tale of adventure, humour and the triumph of the human spirit. It's an experience you'll never forget.